AN OLD-FASHIONED FASHIONED HOMESTEAD

KATIE DOUGLAS

Published by Stormy Night Publications and Design, LLC.
www.StormyNightPublications.com

Cover design by Korey Mae Johnson
www.koreymaejohnson.com

Images by The Killion Group, 123RF/Harris Shiffman, and
123RF/Elena Volkova

1st Print Edition. August 2016

ISBN-13: 978-1535391290

ISBN-10: 1535391294

CHAPTER ONE

I clicked through the job listings with a feeling of despair. Most of the ads on Craigslist were for the sort of jobs I would never even consider, and I was starting to get fatigued just looking at line upon line of 'girls wanted, 18+ for adult work.'

Why was it so hard to find a legitimate job that didn't require a social security number? I was in the USA on a student visa, and I wasn't allowed to work while I was here, but I had another year to go on my Master's degree and I was broke. After page ten of the same slush, I was about to give up. A small ad near the bottom of the page caught my attention; it was posted twelve days ago, but I decided to take a look anyway.

Wanted: help around the house for widower and two boys aged 6 and 4. I need someone to help in the home and look after two boys over the summer on my homestead in Northern California. I have a lot of work to do harvesting and working on my farm, and can't be watching the kids at the same time. Sewing skills and a good work ethic are essential. $100 per week and free accommodation (incl. food, utilities, etc.) if needed. If interested email me.

It was probably already filled, but I decided to shoot him an email anyway. The accommodation would be a definite bonus, since I had to vacate my dorm room in two days' time.

Before I'd applied for any jobs, I had written a cover letter, heavily edited by my roomie Kelly, who was an MBA student.

"There are some key words you need to use, to grab the attention of HR managers," Kelly had said. "Such as 'proactive' or 'motivated self-starter.'"

I reread it, but it just didn't seem appropriate. Feeling guilty, I set the cover letter aside. Perhaps I could use it for a graduate job next year. The task at hand required a more personal touch, so I started again from scratch, then read it aloud to myself in case I had made any mistakes.

"Dear Sir,

I am writing to apply for the vacancy you advertised on Craigslist, requesting someone to look after two children and keep the house in order over the summer. My name is Isabel Sutton, and I am a twenty-four-year-old graduate student (from the UK) studying for my M.A. in anthropology at Berkeley. I have just completed the first year of the Masters' course and am looking for work between now and September when my studies will resume. You mentioned in the advertisement that accommodation would be available, which I would require if it's not too much trouble.

I have attached my Curriculum Vitae and I would like to draw your attention to the experience I had at Sixth Form, when I volunteered as a nursery assistant in my free time for two years, until I went to university (Bristol, England). Since then, I also gained eight months' experience working as a cleaner for an agency in England, from whom I can provide a reference if required.

I am available to start at any time and I have my own car so I can travel at short notice. I look forward to hearing from you soon,

Yours faithfully, Isabel Sutton."

I reread it twice, and although I wasn't completely happy

with the sentence about accommodation, I closed my eyes and clicked 'send,' reminding myself that I wasn't being hired for my writing skills.

I wished I had an allowance from my parents, like Kelly did—she'd gotten both her tuition fees and accommodation paid, and her parents put money in her account every month for food and other expenses. It was *proper* unfair. My mother was a nurse and my dad was… well, currently he was a used carpet salesman (some sort of environmentally friendly startup) but before that he'd been a waiter, a taxi driver, and a train conductor. Job security wasn't his strong point. If it hadn't been for mum's sacrifices, we would have been turned out of our lovely family home years ago.

After the stress of the job search and the relief of finding anything at all to apply for, I closed my laptop and made a cup of tea before looking for any other jobs.

The travel kettle I'd brought from England had a heavy adapter plug on it, and Kelly had joked about how it couldn't brew coffee, but it did make tea. I much preferred to start the day with a nice cup of tea, but teabags were so expensive! So were a lot of my favorite foods—Branston Pickle, French Dijon mustard, and my most loved treat, my Saturday night dinner, a fresh, tender steak. As I squooshed the teabag against the side of the cup, I reflected that I'd spent far too much of my savings on home comforts. I suppose that was how I ended up looking for a job at the last minute, to raise a little cash. It was a good thing I'd acquired a taste for American chocolate or I'd have been bankrupted before Christmas, given my sweet tooth.

Before I had left for America, I had budgeted meticulously, worked sixty hours a week at the cleaning company to save the cash, but there were all those little unexpected costs that had eaten away at two years of money in barely nine months.

I sat down with my finished drink and stared out of the window.

My last anthropology class had been on Friday, and my

studies wouldn't begin again until September. Had I really been in California for a whole year?

The tea mug was barely empty when I saw a reply in my inbox.

Re: Wanted: help around the house for widower and two boys aged 6 and 4.

Excited, I clicked on the message to open it.
He actually got back to me!

Miss Sutton, are you free this afternoon for a telephone interview? Nate.

My heart leapt and I replied quickly.

Sure, call any time.
Izzy.

Less than a minute after I hit send, my phone started beeping.

"Hello?" I answered.

"Is this Isabel Sutton?" A man's voice, deep and unmistakably American, said my name in a way that gave me a slight thrill.

Was this really my potential employer?

"Hi, I mean, um… this is she!" I blustered, trying to remember my manners.

"I'm Nate Byrne, I've just got a few questions to ask," he said.

"Go for it," I said, hoping I wasn't being too casual.

"Have you ever lived on a real homestead, Miss Sutton?" he asked.

"Can you just, um, clarify what a homestead is, please?" I asked, feeling sheepish. The last time I used the word homestead was in an essay during my study of Viking culture, and I was pretty sure that no non-indigenous

American people lived in wattle and daub houses with thatched roofs.

"It's a small farm that's virtually self-sufficient," Nate replied.

"Oh, in England we would call that a smallhold!" It was one of those words that apparently hadn't made it across the Atlantic. "My uncle had one, where he raised chickens, sheep and had an orchard with the most delicious fresh apples."

"Smallhold? That's a great word. So, at my place, we're not totally self-sufficient, but we make most of our food here on the farm. I know I advertised for someone to help around the house—and I do need that—but there are certain times of the year when everyone is expected to pitch in, for example when it's time to harvest the crops or if any of the goats are birthing. Would you have any problems with that, young lady?"

"Actually, Mr. Byrne, it sounds delightful. I used to love visiting my uncle's smallhold. Everything just felt so… refreshing; do you know what I mean?" I thought back to the chickens, and how I used to get so excited when it was time to look for eggs.

"Yeah, I know what you mean. Let's talk about housework for a minute. You said you worked for a cleaning agency for a time?"

"Yes, I was a Millie Maid," I confessed. Would he know what that was? "Blue polyester uniform, driving to people's houses, cleaning up after them. Some of the messes people left were horrific but most people I visited were just too busy to keep their houses in order."

"Why'd you do it? I mean, why would you want to do that sort of job?"

What was that supposed to mean?

"Why wouldn't I want to work as a cleaner?" I was nettled. I had always enjoyed the satisfaction of making someone's house tidy. It pleased me to know that I'd made their life a bit easier, and maybe it was the anthropologist in me but I had felt privileged to see that side of society, to see how people lived from the inside by going into their homes and making them clean and tidy. I had been unprepared for the amount of contempt with which some people treated cleaning staff. If this man had a prejudice, I certainly wasn't going to put myself through cleaning his house.

"I guess I always thought people only cleaned if they weren't able to get another job." He seemed taken aback by my response to his comment.

"Well, some people just like cleaning," I retorted. It was a poor response, but I was mildly annoyed.

Maybe I didn't want to work for this man on his farm after all.

Except… what other job could I get?

"If you liked cleaning so much, why'd you leave, Miss Sutton?" Nate asked.

Touché.

"There was an incident. A man tried to press his advantage while I was making my first visit to his house. Luckily I got away, but it left me shaken and I no longer felt confident going into strangers' homes. The agency was less than understanding, and since I was commencing my final year of university, I decided to focus on my studies." I explained.

"Dear God. I'm sorry." Nate seemed to genuinely care—and after only five minutes on the phone and a couple of emails. Maybe he was just a kind and caring person. I'd not quite gotten used to the American way yet; particularly, the way that Americans seemed to be so warm, so empathic, compared to people in my homeland, where we did not want to pry, lest we be seen as nosy. Perhaps my final project could be a firsthand field study of the differences between ways of life in America and the UK… my mind ticked on for several seconds before I realized there had been silence down the phone that entire time.

"Hello?" I asked, to check we hadn't lost the connection.

"Sorry, I was just thinking," he replied. "So let's put your cleaning knowledge to the test. You're in the middle of vacuuming and the Hoover goes dead. What do you do?"

"Check if it's plugged in properly, check that the wire isn't loose, check I didn't catch the button when I moved it, check the filters and dust bag. Then let you know that your vacuum cleaner is off-color," I said.

"That's great, but I meant what would you do about the floor?" Nate asked.

"Oh, how silly of me! Of course that's what you meant. I'd fetch the dustpan and brush and get it done that way," I said.

"Great, thanks. Okay, next question: you answered the phone and it's a sales call. Someone's knocked on the door and it looks like it's something urgent. What do you do?" he asked.

"Well, that's easy! I'd hang up the phone and answer the door!" I said. "I don't owe the person on the phone anything, and they're wasting my time!"

"That sounds good. Let's just say the salesperson you hung up on calls back and starts berating you for ending the call, they're not letting you get a word in edgewise, what do you do?" he asked.

"I would just hang up again. If they call again, I'd ring one four seven one and get their number, then threaten them with a harassment suit," I said. Would he find that offensive?

"What's one four seven one?" Nate asked, sounding confused.

"Um, the number you dial to find out who just called you so you can return the call," I said, then mentally kicked myself; it probably wasn't the same number here, was it? I had never needed to use it the whole time I'd been in California.

"Oh, star sixty-nine." Nate said. He seemed to be thinking for a moment. "Okay, Miss Sutton, how would you handle a bad date?"

I was nonplussed. What did he want to know *that* for?

Was it even *remotely* any of his business?

I paused for several seconds, wondering whether to answer the question, and if so, what to say.

It would have helped if I'd *been* on any dates in the past few years. Unable to think of a clear, direct answer to such a peculiar question, I just recounted the last date I'd been on.

"The last man I dated was when I was about twenty, so I might be a bit rusty, but the whole evening was a complete disaster from start to finish. He showed up half an hour late, with a dozen chrysanthemums, which he insisted I carry around while we went to dinner then the cinema. I think he wanted people to know that I was his date, which would have been great if he hadn't been on his phone the whole time. At the restaurant, he tried to order for me, but he didn't know me at all, and guessed completely wrong. I am intolerant to lactose, and he ordered me the cheesiest moussaka that I've ever seen, followed by cheesecake with cream. Then he kept making the most awful jokes at my expense. 'Where are you from?' he asked me. 'Originally? Wiltshire,' I replied. 'Oh, we all know about Wiltshire girls,' he said. But then he kept pressing it, over and over. I still haven't a clue what everyone apart from me apparently knows about Wiltshire girls. I eventually told him to shut up, and when we got to the cinema, he ate all the popcorn then left me to make my own way home," I said. I started to blush, aware of the fact that I was probably rambling at this point.

"And what did you do?" Nate asked.

"I got a horrifically expensive taxi. It was late and the buses had finished running. Then when I got home, I found five voicemails on my phone, all from him. Apparently he'd had a great time and couldn't wait to see me again," I said. "Suffice to say, I blocked his number and didn't agree to a second date. Then he showed up at my flat and started banging on the door. I started to become afraid, so I… um… hid in my bathroom until he went away. It wasn't my finest moment, I have to admit."

"Sounds like a bad situation for everyone involved. Although, you know, calling the police when he was at your door might have helped, Miss Sutton," Nate said.

I *knew* that, I just hadn't *done* it.

"So here's a hypothetical for you. You're driving down the road, it's late at night, you're running late and you're alone. You see what looks like a person lying on the side of the road next to a darkened car. What would you do?" he asked.

I frowned. These questions were highly irrelevant; they had nothing to do with getting this job. I contemplated ending the call, but Nate seemed friendly enough, and I really needed the money.

"I would pull over, get out of my car, and check that they were okay. I mean... clearly they're not okay if they're lying on the side of the road, but I'd still need to get an idea of what ailed them. If they were conscious I'd ask them what happened, where were they injured, et cetera. Then I'd ring an ambulance, informing the operator of what was wrong with the person. I'd sit and wait with them until the ambulance arrived, to reassure them that they weren't alone, and I'd make sure they had their keys for their car, because it would add insult to injury if their car got nicked while they were in hospital," I said.

"What if it was pouring down rain?" Nate asked.

"What on Earth has that got to do with anything?" I snorted derisively. "A bit of rain isn't going to ring an ambulance for a person, is it?"

Nate paused for several seconds. I think he was laughing, but covering the receiver with his hand or something. Maybe he thought he had to conduct a serious interview.

"I guess not," he said at length. "Young lady, how much do you drink on an average night out?"

I gave up trying to work out what his angle was, and decided to just go along with it.

"I suppose it depends," I said. "If I was the designated

driver, I would not touch a drop. Lemonade all the way. But if I'm not driving, I'd have two, maybe three drinks, depending on how long we were out for. Pardon me for asking, but what has all this got to do with the job?"

"Would you hire someone to take care of your kids if they went out all night drinking a couple of bottles of wine every evening?" he asked.

"Fair point," I conceded. "Have you any more odd questions?"

"What was the last book you read?" he asked.

I looked at my desk, where *How to Read Ethnography* was stacked on top of *The Social Fabric of the Cook Islands*.

"Do you mean fiction or nonfiction? Because I'm a master's student so I read a lot of stuff for essays and such." I said.

"Let's say fiction."

"Wow, well, it's been a while since I had the time, but I'd say it was *The Lost World* by Arthur Conan Doyle," I answered.

What Nate said next utterly surprised me.

"You got a soft spot for Professor Challenger, Miss Sutton?" he asked.

He had read *The Lost World*? Most people hadn't even heard of it. It was one of my favorites. And, yes, I did have a bit of a thing for the good professor.

"Well, it has turn of the twentieth century manners, long dresses, adventure, gallantry, excitement, live dinosaurs… what's not to love?" I replied. "And I must confess that I do have a certain fondness for him."

I didn't want to tell a complete stranger that my greatest regret in life was being born a hundred years too late. Certainly, I'd not admit—not for all the tea in China—that I would love more than anything to find a strong, decisive man like Professor Challenger, someone who could take charge, a real man with old-fashioned ideals and a firm hand.

This conversation had definitely taken a turn for the personal.

"Can I ask you some questions now?" I asked, feeling vulnerable. How had this man got me thinking about… things so quickly? He was a potential employer, not a date.

My voice of reason stepped in at this point. Had he actually said anything so far to make me think he wanted a relationship? No, I reminded myself. It was my thoughts, my feelings, that had been awakened. He had been polite and professional.

"Fire away, Miss Sutton," he said. His voice was having a strange effect on me now.

Damn, now I needed to think of some questions. Did I have any? My mind was utterly distracted.

"Um… do your children have any medical conditions or disabilities that would require any special care?" I asked.

"No, just two normal American boys who lost their mama way too soon," Nate replied.

"What job do you do?" I asked.

"I'm a farmer these days. Straight out of high school, I joined the army. I was there eight years, until my first son was born."

A soldier? Oh, God, my nipples were straining at my plain white bra and my knickers… would need changing. I didn't expect this conversation to be doing this to me. Was it his voice? The way he kept calling me 'young lady'? Or was I just so sex-starved that I'd throw myself at the first man I saw? What was wrong with me? I needed to snap out of it.

This highly distracting arousal was probably what got me asking my next question quite so bluntly, because I just couldn't concentrate to word it in a tactful manner and I felt it needed saying.

"Are you expecting any sexual favors or ersatz relationship in exchange for money or services?" I asked. I wasn't quite sure what 'ersatz' meant, but I thought it sounded good.

"Nope, not interested in any of that, Miss Sutton. I haven't even met you. But if it goes somewhere…" He left the sentence hanging. I decided to make myself clear.

"I'm not going to work for you if any sort of sex is part of this job description," I said, sounding more confident than I felt. You couldn't be too careful with people you'd met online, right?

"No problem. Any other questions?" he asked, and I felt like he was humoring me.

"Yes. Will the accommodation be in a separate room with a lockable door, and how will you pay me?" I asked.

"Sure, it'll be separate. There's nothing to worry about at my place. I don't exactly live in a palace but it sure ain't a shack either. I can put a lock on the door, no problem, if it makes you feel secure. You'll get paid weekly, one hundred dollars a week into your bank account. Got any more questions, Miss Sutton?" he asked, and I realized he'd stayed calm while I'd been getting stressed out over the nature of this job. The incident at the cleaning company had apparently affected me more than I knew at the time. Or was I just going on the offensive to cover up my own blatant interest in this man? Probably a bit of both. I couldn't be too careful.

This was so humiliating, I was glad he couldn't see me because my face was beetroot.

"No... that's everything," I said. Nate was silent for several seconds. He seemed to be thinking.

"I guess you'll do," he said at length. "Can you start tomorrow?"

"Um... okay," I said. I hadn't expected him to want me to start so soon, but it would certainly solve my little housing problem without me resorting to living in my car. "Where am I going? How far are you from Berkeley?"

"Oh, didn't I post the address? It's Byrne Ranch, it's on route 299, after Big Bar. If you get to Salyer, you've gone too far," he said. "It's about a six-hour drive from 'Frisco, so a bit less from Berkeley. Do you want map coordinates?"

"Map whats? Never mind, don't worry, I'll find it." I wrote down the details he gave me.

"Great, I'll see you at midday tomorrow, then? I'm looking forward to meeting you, Isabel. Don't be late or you'll miss lunch," he added.

For some reason, I wanted nothing more than to eat lunch with this man I'd never met.

I got off the phone and stared into space for long minutes; what was I getting myself into? Why had Nate asked all those bizarre questions? I had been to a lot of job interviews in the past, and none of them had been like that. Was this a scam?

Something in Nate's voice made him sound trustworthy. This was a big risk, but my gut instinct told me it was the right thing to do.

The room was untidy, despite the inner peace I derived from cleaning. I pulled out my two purple suitcases to fill with my belongings. When they were full, I still had things left over. I tried straddling the bigger of the two suitcases to try to get it to zip up. It refused. Wiggling my hips in a most ungainly manner, I finally got it fastened, but looking around the room, I realized I would need to get rid of a few things that I'd accumulated over the past year.

I sifted through my clothes and shoes, and separated some items to take to Goodwill. It was still open, so I drove over at once. When I got back, I tackled the fridge.

By the time I went to sleep, the car was packed and everything was clean and tidy.

In the morning, I got up at half past four, showered, and put on the clothes I'd prepared the night before, then took a last look around my dorm room, my home for the past year. It looked sad and empty without all the usual posters and clutter.

I picked up my remaining things, stuffed them into a plastic bag, and walked out. I posted the key through the slot at the reception desk, so that the receptionist would find it when she arrived in four hours' time. That was it, then, the end of the year.

With a sigh, I pushed the double doors open and stepped

out into the parking lot, gasping at the chilly mist of dawn. This was my favorite time of day, before the town awakened, whilst the day was pregnant with possibilities.

I unlocked my car, a 1992 Volkswagen Rabbit, and got ready for the drive. The engine roared to life and I pulled out of the lot, then after a brief journey through Albany, I was on the freeway, on route to my new job. That was a slightly nerve-racking thought. I'd never just packed up and moved in with a complete stranger like this before. University halls of residence clearly didn't count. Despite how honest Nate seemed, what if this job was a fake? What if Nate had changed his mind since I spoke to him last night? I couldn't afford the petrol to drive seven hours, just to be turned away again.

Was I just looking for things that could go wrong? I tried to distract myself. Irritating pop blared through the speakers after I turned the radio on. When I stopped at some traffic lights, I flicked at the tuning button, and I was soon able to get the station changed to something more civilized. The soft piano and saxophone tones of some jazz music soothed my nerves and I started to enjoy the journey.

I wondered what Nate looked like, whether he was attractive; his voice had sounded older, more mature than the men I was used to spending time around. Most of my coeds were younger and definitely more immature than I was. It was a hazard of being a postgraduate and living on campus.

Nate sounded like a real man.

I imagined him in dirty jeans and a t-shirt with the sleeves cut off, perhaps heaving biceps streaked with oil from fixing a car. I caught my train of thought and chided myself; I hadn't even met him yet, how could I be thinking like this about my future employer? Regardless of what my brain thought, my pussy spasmed at the imagined vision of Nate. I could dream a little.

CHAPTER TWO

It was twelve-fifteen. Where was Isabel? She'd piqued my interest on the phone and I was looking forward to meeting her. I'd set aside most of the day to get her settled. If she'd changed her mind about coming to my farm, the least she could do was call. I had goats to milk, among a whole host of other tasks that needed doing on a daily basis. She'd seemed nice enough when we spoke, if a little reserved, but I was hoping she'd warm up to me.

I went into the kitchen and looked at the phone on the wall. It wasn't anything fancy; it had a speaker button but no answering machine. With its good old-fashioned loud ring, I sure would've heard if she'd tried to call.

"Dad, when are we having lunch?" Mason asked. That was my boy, thinking with his stomach at all times of the day. If it wasn't a request for a meal, he was looking for candy or snacks. I never saw a kid who was so constantly hungry, but my pa told me I was the exact same at that age.

"Soon as Miss Sutton gets here, kiddo, we'll dig in." I said, ruffling his hair. "Go play with your brother while we're waiting, I'm sure she'll be here soon."

It was one o'clock, an hour late, when I heard a car pulling up to the house. I looked out of the kitchen window and got my first glimpse of Miss Sutton.

With her auburn hair and petite figure, she was just about the opposite of my dearly departed Louisa, who had been round and jolly with light blond hair.

Miss Sutton was mighty pretty, but hers was a delicate beauty. She looked like she might break in a strong wind, but if she could take care of the house and the kids, I didn't really mind what she looked like.

I had to admit though, even though I'd never say it to someone I'd just met, there was something attractive about her elfin features.

As she walked toward the house in her floral summer dress, I noticed her gait was very precise. She placed one foot delicately in front of the other. Didn't they teach that to English women in schools or something? All that walking around with a book on their head? I knew nothing about any of it, and I was intrigued. The way she moved was just incredible. Everything about her reminded me of a ballerina.

Shaking my head, I tried to snap out of it. I went to the kitchen door and opened it to greet her.

"Well, hello, Miss Sutton." I said. "I'm Nate Byrne. You're a little late but we've held lunch for you."

She looked surprised.

"I'm so sorry, I didn't want to put you to any trouble," she said.

"Come on in and sit yourself down, Miss Sutton—looks like you've had a long drive," I said, indicating her dust-covered car.

"Thank you. It *was* rather stressful," she conceded.

"Well, I'm glad you could make it. I think we're going to get along just fine." I gave her a warm smile. "However, since we need to start as we mean to go on, I might as well let you know right now that there are rules in this house, and one of them is that we are always on time."

She looked at me sheepishly.

"I know you've only just got here and you didn't know, but I'm letting you know for the future. It's just as important

16

as doing what you say you're going to, or what you've been asked to do. Folk are always polite to each other here, and I won't tolerate shouting or other unpleasantness," I said. "We solve things by talking first and foremost, unless it doesn't get to the bottom of the issue." I paused for a moment, thinking about Miss Sutton's bottom. If I were a betting man, I'd be willing to place a wager that her pert butt had never been spanked in her life. "Do you have any questions about any of that?"

"No," she said, with a slight smile.

I waved to the kitchen table.

"Pick a seat, I'll go get the boys," I said, but before I could take a step toward the living room, Mason and Taylor came into the kitchen.

"Is it lunch now?" Mason asked, eyes hopeful.

"Sure." I replied. "This is Miss Sutton; she is going to be helping out around the house and taking care of you boys while I get work done around the farm. What do you want the boys to call you?"

"Oh, um… I hadn't really thought about it. I suppose it would be best if they just called me Izzy," she said.

I was surprised—she'd seemed so formal, I'd expected her to want them to address her as Miss Sutton. That's how I'd prefer to address her. After all, I didn't want to be too informal with my first and only employee.

"Great. Say hello to Izzy, then, boys," I said.

"Hello, Izzy," Mason said.

"'Lo, Izz," Taylor tried to say. He was still a bit slow to pick up some sounds in new words.

"Hello, Mason and Taylor," she said, with a warm smile that could melt the North Pole.

After we ate lunch, I cleared away the plates so I could show Izzy where everything was in the kitchen.

"Let me give you a tour," I said once the kitchen was tidy.

"You've seen the kitchen. Through here's the living room, or parlor, as y'all call it in Britain," I said, trying to make a joke.

"Actually, we tend to call it the living room as well," she said. "In England, anyway."

I got the feeling I might have offended her.

"Great, well, no confusion then, right?" I said, trying to smooth it over. I couldn't help wondering how she was going to fit in around here.

"Are the boys allowed to play in here?" Izzy asked.

"Yep. Well, unless they're grounded—then they gotta stay in their rooms except for mealtimes and bathroom times," I said. "Let's move on."

I showed her the utility room.

"This is where all the cleaning products are kept, and the vacuum," I said. "If you need anything like that, it's probably in here."

We moved upstairs and I pointed to the closed doors.

"This is my room. That's the boys' room. They're sharing until they're a little older; I think it helps them learn to get along with each other. This will be your room." I showed her the spare room with its white walls and single bed. I hoped she'd like it.

"Thanks. Where's the wardrobe?" she asked. I tried to guess what a wardrobe might be by what was missing from her view of the room.

"Built-in closet, right over here." I replied, moving the bedroom door so she could see.

Apparently that was a wardrobe, because she smiled and nodded.

I noticed she checked the door, and with her nimble fingers she tested the bolt I'd added at her earlier request.

"Let's go outside," I said. "You'll have plenty of time up here when the boys are in bed."

"Where's the bathroom?" she asked, as we went back downstairs.

"Down here." I showed her the bathroom, next to the living room, then led her outside.

"Your garden is beautiful! So many flowers!" she

exclaimed.

I smiled. "It's my pride and joy. When I get the time to work on it, that is. Out here, we've got a few different buildings; the one you need to pay attention to is the barn. It's been damaged by the storm we had two weeks ago, and it's not safe. The boys like to play in there normally, but don't you let them, because I've got repairs to make. That green one is the tool shed, then there's the woodshed, the goat pens, and the chicken shed. We have four goats, eighteen chickens—we sell fresh eggs to a local store to make a profit—and we grow peas, zucchinis, carrots... a whole stack of other vegetables. We generate some of our own electricity and I fixed the water system so we've got fresh, natural drinking water as well. We can't make everything we need, of course; car parts, fabrics and clothing, that sort of thing gets bought from stores. Over here is the orchard. We have cherry and orange trees."

"Wow. That's a lot of fruit trees," she said.

"Fruit's an important part of a balanced diet. The boys are allowed to play outside as long as they don't bother the animals, or get into the vegetable garden," I said. "Especially when the goats are birthing."

"Do they have kids often?" she asked.

"Just once a year. I don't allow it to happen any more 'n' that. Two of them are coming up to it around now though, and the goats are our source of dairy—milk, cheese, butter—so those are in short supply at the moment because I don't allow the pregnant does to give milk for the last two months before they have their kids," I said.

"So what tasks will I be doing on a daily basis—you mentioned that I was to help around the house as well as watch the children," she asked.

"Yeah, I wrote it all down for you. I also included the list of exactly what I want for lunch and dinner every day this week and all the recipes are in the cookbook in the kitchen. Here." I gave her the list. "It's all the jobs that need doing around this place, with when I expect them to be done."

"What happens if they're not?" she asked.

"Then, Miss Sutton, I'll have to put you over my knee and spank you," I said with a twinkle in my eye. I watched her face carefully to gauge her reaction.

She laughed, but she couldn't hide the fact that a crimson blush had spread from the apples of her cheeks across the rest of her face.

I wanted to tease her a little about the color of her face, but I checked myself. I needed to avoid scaring her away. At least she was warming to me now.

Maybe, with time, I might act on my obvious attraction to Miss Sutton, but for now, I would content myself with the knowledge that the boys would be in good hands. I figured she wasn't going to let them run wild.

"If you spank me, Mr. Byrne, you'd better be prepared for the consequences," she said. I couldn't figure out if she meant she'd throw herself at me or call the cops. I changed the subject quickly; this conversation was getting off topic.

"Right, dinnertime. I was going to make burger and fries; do you know how to make homemade fries, Miss Sutton?" I asked.

"Yes, peel a potato, cut it into chip shapes and either fry it or brush with oil and bake," she replied.

"Great, I look forward to seeing how it turns out. I'll be ready to eat at six."

"That's rather early, isn't it?" she asked.

"Usually, we eat at five-thirty, so the boys are in bed at seven, but I thought I'd push it back a little since you were late getting here," I said. She nodded.

"Okay. It's your house, after all," she conceded.

"Do you have a cell phone, Miss Sutton?" I asked her. She nodded.

"Take my number, so you can reach me if you need anything. Usually a shout's enough, but there are some parts of the farm where it's hard to hear sometimes," I said.

"Thank you." She put the number into her phone.

"Call me if you need any help at all," I said.

She nodded.

I left her to it, wondering whether she could cook real American food.

Three hours later, I was pleasantly surprised. She had not only managed to make the fries but also to work on her initiative and prepare some vegetables. She had set everything out in bowls in the center of the table, and there was a plate, a knife, and a fork for each of us.

"This looks incredible." I said, taking a seat. The boys were already seated.

"Right, folks, let's dig in," I said.

The food was great, but I was glad I'd eased her into it all this afternoon and taken the time to explain things to her. I didn't want to overwhelm her with life here on the farm, which could get pretty intense at times.

• • • • • • •

That night, I showed her how I put the boys to bed.

"Taylor likes to go to bed with his cuddly dinosaur. He can't sleep without it and sometimes he loses it. Mason is usually pretty good at just going to sleep. I'm pretty sure he could sleep through a volcano," I joked.

Miss Sutton put her hand over her mouth.

"Do you have them here? Volcanoes, I mean?" she asked. She looked so serious when she said it that I just wanted to bundle her up in a blanket and kiss her all over.

"No, there are no volcanoes here. It was just a joke," I said.

"Oh, good." She looked visibly relieved.

I walked her to her room once the boys were in bed. "Good night, Miss Sutton," I said, trying to stay on formal terms.

"Good night, Mr. Byrne." She let herself into her room and closed the door behind her. A second later, I heard the bolt slide into place.

As I went to my own bed, I wondered how she was going to fit in here. Would she adjust to our way of life? I fell asleep thinking about it all.

• • • • • • •

The morning was already bright when I awoke. By the time I was downstairs, she was already making breakfast.

"Morning, Mr. Byrne," she said cheerfully.

"You're up early, Miss Sutton." I was surprised.

"The list said breakfast was served at half past six. That meant, if it took me half an hour to prepare breakfast at a leisurely pace, that I would need to rise at half past five. So I did." She said it as if it was the most obvious thing in the world. "I've always been an early riser."

"Great. I kinda expected to have to wake you," I said in amazement.

She placed four plates of food on the table.

"I'm going to go and get the boys," she said, and disappeared. I was impressed. When none of them appeared after ten minutes, I went to the foot of the stairs.

"Taylor, Mason, get yourselves down here, we've got breakfast to eat!" I shouted up to them.

They were down in under a minute, followed by Miss Sutton, who looked sheepish.

"Sorry, I was unsure about how to get them out of bed," she said.

I was surprised.

"Usually, I just tell them it's time to get up, and they get up," I said. "Boys, you got to behave for Miss Sutton, you hear?" I gave them a stern look. They both nodded, pretending to be innocent.

I decided to see whether they did anything similar again before I intervened—she needed a chance to learn how to get them to behave, so I wouldn't need to step in all the time.

After breakfast, I stood up to get on with the day's work.

"I'm going to milk the goats, then I've got some trees to cut down on the edge of the property, they got damaged in that storm I told you about yesterday," I said.

"Okay."

"You remember what I said about the barn yesterday?"

"Yes," she said, nodding.

"Great, so don't let the boys play in there," I reminded her. "If anyone comes to the door, you just come get me and I'll talk to them, but it's unlikely that will happen."

"Got it."

"See you round lunchtime then," I said, and left her to it.

Despite my reservations, she seemed to know what to do. I went to milk the goats with a spring in my step.

CHAPTER THREE

When Nate left I realized that while he'd been talking, all I'd been able to concentrate on was his voice. I was so busy listening to the sound of it that I hadn't heard everything he'd said, but I got the impression he'd told me already the day before, so what was there to worry about?

The morning passed fairly uneventfully. I played with Mason and Taylor in the living room after I found them arguing about a toy, and then I put the TV on for them to watch while I prepared lunch.

I was doing this!

At lunchtime, Nate returned from his work.

"How have you been getting on?" he asked.

"Izzy played jungles with us!" Taylor said.

"She was a lion!" Mason said. "But I was an alligator."

"Sounds like you had a great time. I think Miss Sutton is doing a great job taking care of you two, but I'm wondering if she'll find the time to clean my kitchen this afternoon?" He smiled and raised an eyebrow rakishly. "It was on your list of things to do this morning but it sounds like you were busy."

I couldn't help thinking he wasn't happy that I'd spent the morning playing with my charges. Isn't that what I was here for? To look after them? It was only my first day and I didn't want to sound whiny so I decided to let it go.

"Of course," I said.

"You've still got dinner to make as well, young lady, did you get a chance to look at the recipe?" he asked.

I shook my head.

"From what I've seen, you know your way around a kitchen, but it will be ready on time, won't it?" he asked.

"Yes, it will." I didn't know what else to say. I could handle dinner for four people.

"Great."

After we all ate, Nate left and I got on with cleaning the kitchen. I still hadn't so much as glanced at the recipe. At about three o'clock, Mason and Taylor appeared in the doorway.

"Can we go outside?" Taylor asked.

"Yes, I don't see why not," I said. After all, fresh air was good for growing boys.

They went off outside to play, and I scrubbed the oven, which was on the list of tasks. Arms aching and covered in grease, I finished an hour later and, after a good wash in the kitchen sink, I looked at the recipe.

Flour, butter, vegetable stock…

I looked at the ingredients. They were all things I'd heard of, and I found the flour and butter easily. I measured them out, using the measuring cups, and put them in a pan. I drained the vegetables and set aside the liquid they'd been cooked in—that would be the vegetable stock. The recipe had said make a roux, but I didn't know what that was, so I just poured everything into a saucepan and tried to mix it together.

It was a disaster. There were blobs of flour floating at the top in those clumps that turn powdery when you try to mix them. There were blobs of butter that would not mix with anything else. I vaguely remembered from school cooking lessons that a roux was something to do with cheese sauce, so I tried putting some cheese in, thinking it might melt and bind everything together. It just made things worse. Now there were blobs of cheese that hadn't melted properly and underneath it all, the vegetable stock, looking deathly pale, was stubbornly refusing to thicken.

At home, I would have thrown it into the blender then microwaved it until it looked right, but here, there was no blender, nor a microwave. I got the whisk out to try to smooth it and turned the heat up to melt the butter and cheese.

"Izzy?" Mason was at the doorway again.

"What is it?" I asked, looking round.

"It's raining. Can we play in the barn?" he asked.

I was so busy with the food that I just wanted the children to play quietly somewhere and not distract me. The barn sounded like a great idea. They'd be out of the rain but still out of the house.

"Yes, go and play in the barn. I'll give you a shout when it's dinnertime," I said, and turned back to the cooking. When I managed to part the liquid vegetable stock, I saw that some of the ingredients had burned to the bottom of the pan due to the higher heat. And still the sauce wouldn't thicken.

I felt like I was auditioning for *I Love Lucy*; all I needed was a top-loading washing machine spewing foam everywhere.

I set the pan aside and started again. That pan was going to require some serious scrubbing, and time was running out. The meat was nearly cooked in the freshly cleaned oven.

I whipped out my phone and checked the Internet to see how to make a roux.

Add butter and flour to a pan on a medium heat and mix, it will form lumpy balls, cook until lightly brown.

Oops.

I was just measuring out more flour when Nate put his

head around the door.

"Hey, just checking in, how's it going?" he asked, and I was just hoping to convince him of my Domestic Goddessitude when he added, "What's that burning smell?"

"That's the first attempt at the stew base," I said, feeling stupid.

"It went wrong? How?" Nate asked.

"The instructions said to make a roux. I didn't know what that was," I confessed.

"Why didn't you call me?" he asked. "I could have explained in seconds."

"I was trying not to disturb you and by the time I realized it had gone wrong, it was already looking like that," I said.

That might have been the end of it, had he not peered into the pan.

"Miss Sutton, why is there cheese in this discarded stew base?" he asked, raising an eyebrow. I felt so embarrassed.

"I just... thought it might help." I wanted him to understand that I was trying my best, but if he was going to leave recipes using fancy *cordon-bleu* words then it could hardly be helped if things went wrong.

"Have you ever eaten a stew with goat's cheese in it? There's a reason nobody puts that in stew, young lady," Nate said.

"Look, I didn't know that, okay?" I started to push back. Couldn't he see how much time I'd spent trying to fix it?

"Food in this house is valuable, young lady. I make nearly everything that we eat here. The butter, the cheese, the vegetables are all usually homemade—and we are in very short supply of dairy right now, because two of my goats are heavily pregnant. The point is, I cannot afford to waste food." He didn't sound angry but I still felt like I'd let him down. "Next time, instead of wasting ingredients, if you don't know how to do something, I expect you to ask me for help. Do I make myself clear?"

"Yes, and I'm sorry," I said, and I meant it. "I had no idea that a bit of flour and butter was going to cause such a problem."

"Think about it, Miss Sutton. Where are you going to get the vegetable stock from to make the new stew? You either have to cook up more vegetables, in which case there's now more vegetables than we need, so some of it will be wasted, or we have to go without sauce," Nate said.

"What if I used the juices from the meat?" I asked. "People make beef stock and chicken stock all the time, right?"

"You can do that this time, but get it right next time," Nate said.

I nodded. First time, next time, this time, on time—time was all he seemed to think about.

"Do you need any help with the roux?" he asked.

"Flour, butter—"

Crash!

"What was that?" Nate held up a hand. I shook my head. I knew as much as he did—a loud crash had come from outside. Then I realized what it was.

"Oh, my God, the boys!" I cried. We ran out to the barn. Mason was standing in the doorway crying. I picked him up as Nate ran past me.

Inside the barn, the hayloft had collapsed.

"Help! I'm stuck!" Taylor's voice called plaintively.

"I'm coming Taylor, just hang tight!" Nate called. I watched him lift the fallen wood—half of the platform from the hayloft, I think—and Taylor crawled out from under it.

"Are you hurt?" Nate asked his son as he hurried him out of the barn.

"No, daddy, I'm fine, the hay broke my fall," Taylor said.

"Taylor seems unharmed," I interjected, glad both boys were safe.

"What were you two doing in the barn? I've told you not to go in there until it's fixed up," Nate said.

That was when I remembered that he'd told me the boys weren't allowed in the barn.

I felt mortified.

"Izzy said we could go in," Mason said earnestly.

"Is this true, Miss Sutton?" The look Nate gave me could have peeled paint.

"Mason asked while I was sorting out the sauce, and I wasn't really paying attention. It seemed like a good idea for them to play somewhere out of the rain and—" I tried to stammer an explanation, but Nate stopped me.

"No," he said. "I will talk to you about this after dinner, Miss Sutton."

He walked toward the chicken coops, leaving Mason, Taylor, and me standing in the rain outside the injured barn.

"Indoors, you two, come on." I deposited Mason on his own two feet and took them back to the house, where I insisted that they play in the living room until dinner was served.

Despite the chicken stock making a delicious stew, of which I was very proud, dinner was a subdued affair in which none of us really spoke.

Mason clearly knew he shouldn't have asked me if he was allowed to do something that his father had explicitly told him not to do; he had apologized to me twice while I was serving dinner and was very quiet throughout the meal. Taylor was sleepy from the day's adventure. I knew I had badly upset Nate, and he spoke to me only when he had to, in a measured voice that seemed to be taking a lot of control.

"Can you please pass the salt, Miss Sutton," he said, after seeing that it was out of his reach.

"Here you go." I handed it to him. He avoided my fingers.

I didn't know how to make this right. I was here to primarily take care of the boys and I hadn't done that. After I'd cleared up the dinner things, I went to find him. He was in the living room. The boys were playing in their room.

"Miss Sutton, when I employed you, you assured me that you knew how to look after children and take care of the house. Today, you put my boys in serious danger. Since my wife died two years ago, they are all that I have. If anything happened to them…" He trailed off, squeezing his fist tight with emotion.

"Look, I really am sorry," I said. "I can't be in two places at once."

"It's not about being in two places at once. Young lady, I explicitly told you not to let the boys play in the barn. It was so important, I told you twice. You clearly didn't listen, or maybe you thought that it wasn't important enough to you to remember. As soon as my back was turned, the boys were in there, and part of the structure came down. Taylor had a very lucky escape today. I now don't know if I can trust you with my children, Miss Sutton, and I will not tolerate such a shocking disregard for my instructions." He looked disappointed and angry. "So I am going to give you a choice. You can either leave and find some other job to support you for the summer, or you can accept a spanking from me after the boys are asleep."

I stared at him and tried not to let my reaction show on my face. Bloody hell. Was he serious? I couldn't remember ever being spanked in my life, even when I stayed with my strict grandmother.

I needed this job though; what other job could I get on a student visa, with no Social Security number?

More than that, I felt that if I left now, it was as good as saying that I didn't give a toss about what I did. And I most certainly did care. I felt awful and knew I had to make this right.

"I will accept a spanking," I said.

"Thank you for letting me know, Miss Sutton," he said.

I hurried away and busied myself with the washing up, taking care not to break any of the plates.

After the boys were in bed, I went back downstairs. Ever since Nate's ultimatum, I had been dreading this moment.

"Come here, young lady," he said.

I stepped forward slowly. My legs had turned to jelly.

When I was closer, he reached out and took my hand; the next thing I knew he was pulling me over his knee.

This was actually happening. I felt my heartrate quicken in anticipation of what was about to happen.

Once I was in position, he started straight away, bringing his hand down over my thin floral skirt. At first, I thought I could handle this easily, it was no worse than the tingle of my regular Brazilian wax, but it built up to the point where my bottom was stinging badly under his hand. I tried to keep quiet because the boys were upstairs and I didn't want to worry them, but seriously, this was burning.

"Please, I've learned my lesson. I'm so sorry. I'll never do anything like that again," I tried to reassure Nate that he could stop now.

"I decide when you've learned your lesson. You need this spanking, Miss Sutton," Nate said.

I squeezed my fists into tiny balls. I couldn't take much more of this.

A short moment later, he stopped.

"Thank goodness. That was getting most unpleasant," I said, trying to get up, but Nate held me fast.

"That was just the warm-up, Miss Sutton," he said, then to my disbelief he flipped up my skirt and pulled my knickers down, and recommenced spanking me.

I kicked my legs and tried to wiggle free. This was too far.

"Let me go!" I protested. "It hurts!"

"Young lady, if you continue trying to get out of your punishment, I'll have to use my belt," he said, continuing to spank me. The fire in my bottom was getting worse and worse.

"You're hurting me!" I reiterated.

"It's a punishment spanking, Miss Sutton, it's supposed to hurt," he said. "I am sorry that it has come to this, young lady, but you need to learn your lesson."

I kicked wildly.

"Do you want to leave and find another job, Miss Sutton?" he asked.

"Please, no, I want to stay here," I whimpered.

"All right, Miss Sutton, you leave me no choice. After I've finished your hand spanking, you will also feel my belt. I was not going to, but you are not accepting your spanking. If you will not accept your punishment, you might as well leave in the morning," he said.

Oh, God, I couldn't leave.

I took a deep breath and tried to accept that this was happening whether I wanted it to or not. I did deserve it. The boys could have been killed or gravely injured.

It stung so badly though! More than that, it made me feel vulnerable.

Soon, I was crying. Nate's boys were all he had, and I'd put them in danger. I deserved all this and more. I cried and cried as he spanked me, until at last he stopped and rubbed my bum cheeks. The soothing feeling was unbelievable.

"Up you get, Miss Sutton, and kneel against this chair." He got up out of the seat and I knelt down, my face in the cushion. He must have heard me crying but I didn't want him to see.

There was the unmistakable sound of a belt being unfastened.

My bottom was still sore from the spanking; how much worse was this going to get?

As the first whack hit my left cheek, I gripped the cushion tightly and tried hard not to move. The second blow made contact with my right cheek, and I wanted to jump up and grab my sore bottom. Nate kept bringing his belt down on my bottom, and I just cried and cried. Finally, I went limp, and didn't even try to resist.

When he stopped, he sat down and pulled me into an embrace. He rubbed my stinging behind and rubbed my back.

"Shh shh. It's all right. It's all right." He soothed me with his hands and his words. "You took it well and I forgive you. It's all over now, Miss Sutton, and there's nothing to worry about."

I felt like I could just melt in his arms, despite the pain

in my bum.

"I'm sorry for what I did," I said, and while I had meant it earlier, I *really* meant it now, in a new and deeper way.

"I know, Miss Sutton," he said. "Now, it's long past your bedtime, so go on up to bed, get your rest, and let's start tomorrow with a clean slate."

I nodded, wiping away my tears, and I went, carefully, up to bed.

In the sanctity of my own room, I lay down on my bed, flat on my tummy, and tried to put my thoughts in order. The California summer night was enough of a blanket for me just now, and I reflected that an Alpine winter night would be really, really nice for my poor, burning bum.

Nate hadn't been nasty or sharp. He had waited until he was no longer angry, although he wasn't devoid of emotion of course. I never felt that this was supposed to harm me, so much as to correct me. He had reassured me afterwards, and I'd felt so secure, so safe, and so certain that this punishment was over, that he wouldn't hold my transgressions against me afterwards.

Then there was the fact that I was now, not to put too fine a point on it, somewhat aroused by the events of the evening. I went to sleep trying to figure out why I had felt like that, and how I felt toward Nate. It was undeniable that he had awoken something in me.

CHAPTER FOUR

The morning after I'd spanked Miss Sutton was a fine one. I came downstairs, hoping everything was now straightened out between us, and that she bore me no grudge for what I'd had to do. I wanted everyone in my house to get along and be happy. She had made the breakfast again, I was pleased to see, and now she seemed to be trying to work up the nerve to get the boys out of bed. I decided to give her some pointers so she could get a handle on the situation. It was no use having someone around the house—no matter how much I liked them—who couldn't pull her weight. She sighed heavily, and I put my hand on her shoulder to reassure her.

"What's the matter?" I asked her.

"I'm just steeling myself to go and get Mason and Taylor out of bed," she replied.

"What, exactly, are you having trouble with?"

"I don't know, I suppose I feel like I'm being harsh when I have to persist, when they don't just do what I ask them to."

I sighed. She'd clearly never had kids of her own. I wanted to help but I couldn't do this for her—she needed to learn, just like the boys did.

"Listen, Miss Sutton—Isabel. Kids are not like adults. They need to be reminded of things over and over before they will do them. Half the time they don't actually take in what you're saying. It's important to persevere with them, and to be consistent. That helps them have structure. Why don't you spend some time after breakfast—no more than a half hour, let's say—thinking about how you could balance your housework with watching the boys? Maybe you could research on the Internet? You seem to like doing that to find answers to things," I suggested.

She nodded. "Why can't you get them out of bed?"

"Well, I can, but don't forget, young lady, I did employ you to do this work to take some of the pressure off me. I've got a lot to do around the place that keeps me busy all day, especially just now because I've got so many things to catch up with—all the little jobs I haven't been able to do while I didn't have anyone to help out, such as repairs to things. The place is practically falling down," I joked. "Also you need to build a good relationship with them so they learn to listen to you, otherwise what will you do when I'm not close enough to the house to help out?"

She nodded.

"I'm sorry." She looked so damn vulnerable when she said it. My heart melted again.

"Don't be sorry, you're not in trouble, Miss Sutton, I just need you to know that you've got your work to do, and I've got mine. At least give yourself a chance. Work on getting into a routine with the boys for the rest of the week—you'd be really helping me out. If you're truly unable to get them out of bed still, after a week, I'll take over that task and find you something else you can be doing." I wanted her to try. She was an intelligent girl—she was doing a Master's at Berkeley, after all, so I was pretty confident that she could figure this out.

She skipped off to get the boys out of bed, and I hoped my pep talk had got her fired up to feel more positive; half her problem seemed to be that she just had such a low opinion of her own abilities.

I intended to help her change that. Not that I planned to go easy on her either.

When she returned with the kids, I smiled at the three of them.

"Thank you." I wanted her to see that she'd done a good job, and I didn't want the boys to know they were causing stress, so I didn't say anything more. I gobbled my breakfast down, thinking that if Miss Sutton could just keep the boys out of trouble and make food appear for the next couple of days, I had a pretty good chance of fixing all the fencing that was in disrepair around the property.

I headed out to the toolshed to get my supplies, mentally checking off which of the fences I was going to fix first.

That was odd; the shed door seemed to be sticking.

I examined the door and found that the wood had got waterlogged and had swelled at the top; it must've been due to the storm that damaged the barn. Great, something else that needed fixing. I strong-armed it open and propped it wide with a stick. It would have to be added to my floating list of jobs that needed doing around the place. At this rate, I'd need to do a total rebuild of the whole place in six months' time.

$$\bullet \ \bullet \ \bullet \ \bullet \ \bullet \ \bullet \ \bullet$$

At Nate's suggestion, I did a quick search online on my phone to get an overview on how to get children to behave. I think my main problem was that I hated telling them what to do. Having found a few handy tips, I ate my breakfast in double time to make sure I'd be done before the boys ate theirs.

Nate left, and I addressed my two charges.

"Today I've got some very important grownup jobs for you to do. They're so important, I think you two would be the best boys to do them for me. Taylor, I'd like you to sweep the kitchen floor with the middle-sized brush, and

Mason, can you clean the table for me, please? It will need wiping with a wet cloth. Do you think you can both do that?" I asked.

"Of course I can!" Taylor said.

"Me too," Mason said.

"Bet you can't!" Taylor said.

"Pop your plates in the sink and get cracking for me, please. Who can finish the fastest and do the best job?"

I was surprised that turning it into a bit of a competition got them fired up, but it did—they must have been just the right age—and soon I was free to put the kitchen in order without splitting my attention. Instead of slowing me down, the boys were helping me! It seemed so simple now it was working.

It had been a promising, sunny day when I had got up, and as we cleaned the kitchen the sky decided it could no longer contain itself. Rain blotted out the landscape and made a *twink-twink* noise as it hit the metal roof of the porch.

The boys looked glum.

"Now what can we do?" Taylor asked.

"Let's draw some pictures on this lovely clean table," I said. We searched the boys' bedroom until we found colored pencil crayons, felt-tip pens, and some paper.

We spent the day drawing and coloring, the boys both behaving beautifully. I got the dinner in the oven while I kept an eye on the boys, then I sat back down with them to make sure they knew I was still paying attention. I felt like I just needed a chimney sweep to turn up and duet some catchy musical numbers with me, and I could change my name to Mary Poppins at this rate.

As if on cue, Nate came in, covered in rain, mud, oil, and goodness knows what else. There were even a couple of chicken feathers in his hair. He looked miserable, and for a moment I was afraid he was going to spank me again, but when he focused on my little playgroup at the kitchen table, his frown turned into a wistful smile.

He closed the door behind him and peeled off layers of

soaking clothing.

"It's raining," he said. I laughed; it was a bit of an understatement.

"Stating the obvious," I replied, knowing he'd done it to get a laugh.

"This sure looks like fun, can I join in?" he asked.

"Of course you can," I replied sweetly. "Just as soon as you've had a nice warm shower and got those chicken feathers out of your hair."

He instinctively reached up and grabbed at a piece of hair, and pulled a chunk of mud out of it. The chicken feathers, having avoided retrieval, still sat unashamedly matted into his hair.

"What on Earth have you been doing?" I asked.

"Mending fences," he replied. "I'm going to go and wash up."

I had a moment of confusion, wherein I looked at the clean dishes on the draining board, then back at Nate. Then I remembered. 'Wash up' meant 'to clean yourself' in America, not 'wash the dishes.' I giggled at the idea of Nate, in this state, trying to wash anything other than himself.

"What're you giggling about?" he asked, an amused look on his face.

I explained.

"Well, since it's your job to wash up, maybe you can wash me up, young lady," he said suggestively.

The mental image of Nate in the shower, muscles covered in bubbles, all that steamy warm running water… I blushed furiously. By the time I'd thought of a retort, he'd gone.

I was so distracted that I sat back down with the boys and returned to drawing for twenty minutes or so.

"Is that something burning again, Miss Sutton?" Nate asked, now clean and dry.

I leapt up and ran to the oven. The food was fine.

"You got some mighty fine pictures here, I think these deserve a special place on the fridge!" Nate said, admiring the blobby splodge drawings that the boys had done. He took the pictures reverentially and attached them to the fridge with some magnets.

I watched this little ritual in amazement. He was so good with the boys, and clearly cared about them a lot. For some reason, that made my heart melt.

• • • • • • •

After dinner, I got the boys to go to bed in good order then came back downstairs. At some point in the evening the treacherous rain had thinned out then stopped completely.

"You want a beer?" Nate asked, opening the fridge.

"Yes, please," I replied.

We went out onto the porch and sat in the wicker chairs that lived out there.

"So why did you come to California?" Nate asked me as we sipped beer on the porch.

"I'd be lying if I said it was cheaper or easier to be out here than to stay at home," I said. "I suppose I just wanted to travel a bit before I settled down."

"I came out here six years ago, just after Louisa had given birth to Mason. The army was my life since I was eighteen, but it was starting to look less appealing, and my parents had just moved out here for their retirement—I was born in Montana but they wanted sunshine and waves and no more obligations. I just wanted to be able to take care of my family, you know? See them grow up, be there for them, that sorta thing. I had a lot of cash saved from two tours of Iraq and one of Afghanistan. You don't spend much when you're out there, and army life's pretty well subsidized anyway—so I bought a farm," he said.

"You must have seen some things on tours," I said. It was nice to hear more about him.

"Yeah, sometimes you're amazed by the inhuman things people do to each other, and sometimes you're blown away by the loyalty and kindness in the world." Nate swigged his beer. "You see things that you can never talk about with anyone, and things that you never thought could happen. I think it's a good life, on the balance of it. Gets you out of the sort of nowheresville I was living in as a kid, and you see and do things you never would have seen or done in the civilian world. I've got so many skills that I use every day that I learned in the army. It's pretty cool, but I wouldn't go back. I want to stay with my boys. I crave certainty these days."

"I understand," I said. "I lost everything in the floods in 2007. Most of the south of England was underwater, for weeks, and the rain kept coming. We were lucky—we had relatives we could stay with in Wales—but when we went back… My family's home was destroyed. The furniture and walls were covered in brown sludge; looters had broken in and taken anything that was above the waterline. The rest was ruined, and the photographs were the worst. The laptops were stolen and even the photos in boxes got soaked with the horrible brown gloop. When you live like that for a while, never knowing if you can go home again, unsure whether everything will return to normal, it does leave you shaken. Now, when I see heavy rain for more than a day or two, I start to get scared."

"Well, there's nothing to fear where we live—I chose a plot on purpose that doesn't flood," Nate assured.

"Is this your whole plan?" I asked, then thought I'd sounded a bit harsh. "To farm, I mean."

"No," he said, knocking back some more beer. "I always wanted to have a yacht and sail around the world. I figured what with Louisa getting badly seasick and disliking boats besides, that once the boys were born that was it. The first six months after she died, all I could think of was that I wanted her back. My parents took the boys for the longest time because I was just so… destroyed. I'd found my love, we'd made it work… then she got taken away by some bastard driver whose phone call was more important than my Louisa's life. How could the world work like that? I was filled with anger, sorrow, and a lot of other stuff besides. I just wanted her back. As time went on, I began to accept what had happened. I learned to live again, that life went on. That first year without Louisa was harder than being in Iraq, because when I was deployed, I knew I would see Louisa at the end of it. Trouble is, life doesn't stop just because you've lost something precious."

When I looked at him, I saw a flash of the pain that losing his wife had caused him, but then it was gone again.

"What did you do?" I asked.

"I put myself back together and I carried on. It's all a person can do," he said. I nodded. When I thought about it, he was right; that was all that anyone could do.

The conversation had taken a turn for the morose, and I was eager to cheer Nate up, so I tried to think of something to say.

"If you did get your yacht, and you could go anywhere in it, where would you go?" I asked.

Apparently this was the right topic, and his eyes lit up as he thought about it.

"Hawaii," he said. "For starters. Then on to Tahiti and Papua New Guinea."

"What about Easter Island, with all the giant wooden heads?" I asked.

"That'd be pretty cool, although it's a bit out of the way."

"I always wanted to go to New Zealand and Australia," I said. "I'd love to just see it with my own eyes." I realized I'd gotten ahead of myself. This was his dream yacht journey we were talking about, not my travel plans!

"You ever been to a Pacific island?" he asked. I imagined the two of us on some white sandy beach, palm trees mandatory, swimwear optional, waves lapping at our toes as we just spent time together on the sand.

Paradise.

"No, I've never been," I said.

"One day I'd like to take you along," Nate said, and I

thought he was seeing the same mental image as I was until he added, "to keep an eye on the boys, of course."

I nodded. Of course.

"If you bought a yacht, what would you do about the boys' schooling?" I asked.

"Home-schooling. Only, it'd be more... yacht schooling, because we'd be on a yacht," Nate said, and I giggled at his word play. Oh, dear, I had it *bad*.

"You'd need someone who could organize the children and their learning so you could focus on route planning, sailing, and such," I said.

"You're right—an elementary teacher would be ideal. At least for the first few years," Nate agreed.

That was completely not *what I meant, Nate. I meant* me!

I tried to think about how to approach it without seeming too eager. I didn't want him thinking I had the wrong reasons. *Perish the thought...*

"You'd have to get someone who wouldn't mind being replaced when the boys reached a high school level of understanding at that rate," I said. "Because you would probably go for long periods of time with no Internet, so they wouldn't just be able to look things up. You'd be better off going for someone with a good general level of education, perhaps someone who has studied a broad subject with a lot of science, history, geography and literary traditions in it." I added pointedly, "An anthropology graduate, for example?"

He looked at me as if he was seeing me in a new light. I felt uncomfortable. Had I gone too far?

"Sorry. It was just a thought," I said, trying to backpedal. I sometimes wished I could hit the 'undo' button to fix real life.

"There's no need to apologize," Nate said. He held my gaze with his strong, brown eyes, and leaned in toward me. I had the impression that he was about to kiss me, and I opened my mouth slightly. I wanted to let him in.

"Dad!" The porch door slammed open.

We flew apart as if we'd been shocked, and I felt like an actor in a Bhangra movie.

"Why are you out of bed, Taylor?" Nate asked kindly.

"Mason's got my Rarr-Rarr and he won't give her back!" Taylor said.

"Why's Mason got your dinosaur?" Nate asked, getting to his feet and ushering Taylor back into the house.

"Don't know," Taylor said. "But she's mine! Can't sleep now!"

Nate smiled apologetically at me and followed Taylor upstairs. I noticed the beer bottles were empty so I tidied up and went inside to wash the evening's cups before bed.

The evening had taken a turn for the... what? It had become quite confusing. I was certainly in the dark about whether Nate had been about to kiss me or not, let alone his motivations for doing so. Was it going to be a kiss between two friends? Had he just been taking advantage of the moment? Or was there something more going on here? It was all rather mysterious. I looked down and spotted that I'd washed the same cup twice.

How could I know how Nate felt about me? He was concerned for my wellbeing, albeit in an authoritative sort of way, and I did seem to be very preoccupied with making him happy. I wanted to please him. Did he feel anything toward me, other than the usual relationship between employer and employee? Every so often I saw a glimmer of something more, then it disappeared again, lost in the day's events.

I went to bed feeling thoroughly confused.

CHAPTER FIVE

I got the boys to settle pretty well in the morning. They got up with the smallest amount of encouragement and generally seemed eager to help with some of the housework; getting them out from under my feet and meaning I spent less time on my list of tasks.

While they cleaned up, I made some dough for bread and set it to rise, which would take some time.

"You boys have done such a good job making this kitchen look spotless, you can go to your room and play now," I said.

"Can we play outside later?" Mason asked.

"Hmm… if you're good and stay away from that barn," I said.

"We will, I promise!" Mason said.

Taylor nodded. I'm not sure he really understood what a promise was, but he certainly wanted to go outside in the sunshine.

"I'll wait to see what the weather's doing, it seems fairly windy at the moment," I said. "Go and play upstairs for now."

The boys went off and I checked my list.

Dusting.

Ugh, I hated it. For some reason Nate had decided to write: *Carefully. Use a stepladder*, next to the instruction to dust. As if he couldn't trust me or something.

Maybe I could get through it quickly. I pulled out a duster and surveyed the living room. It didn't seem too dusty.

I started with the front of the bookcase, then worked my way around the room: the front of the television table, the top of the TV, the screen. I felt like one of those cartoon princesses who sings and all her friends are bluebirds. Only in this case the bluebirds were china ornaments so they couldn't join in a duet.

I spun around in a circle and flourished the duster as I spun. Doing a little waltz, I tickled the top of the fireplace but I couldn't quite reach. I knew that his little note had told me to find the stepladder but I really couldn't be bothered so I just pulled one of the chairs across then spun again, adding a little jump, hoping to leap onto the chair and catch the mantelshelf in one fluid movement. I was a regular ballerina, or so I thought.

Smash!

I miscalculated. I landed on the edge of the chair with one foot, and it toppled. As I waved my arms to stop myself from falling I caught one of the ornaments, then I smacked into the stone fireplace with my shoulder and slid to the floor, feet caught up in the back of the chair. I disentangled myself from the chair and surveyed the damage.

The little bluebird had hit the bloody fireplace when I knocked it over. Its head had come away from its body, both its legs had snapped, leaving its disembodied feet standing on the little ornamental branch, and its tail was chipped. To add injury to insult, my shoulder was screaming at me.

What had I done? My mood comprehensively killed, I collected the parts of the poor injured bluebird in a sheet of newspaper and gently placed it on the kitchen table.

It definitely looked fixable, and I thought if I hurried I could probably get away with it before Nate found out.

After all, he had written: *Dust carefully, use a stepladder*. Dancing and jumping around waving a duster did not, I was absolutely certain, qualify as careful dusting, and there was no universe where a chair was a stepladder. I rubbed my shoulder; it was a little sore from where I'd hit the fireplace during my tumble. What if that had been my head?

Why hadn't I just done it properly, *then* had a bit of a dance while I was doing something more robust like the vacuuming? Nobody ever damaged a carpet by dancing on it. Well, unless they were wearing those really spiky golfing shoes, but that was beside the point.

I had to fix this before he found out what I'd done. I was going to need some glue. Strong glue. Where would Nate keep his glue?

I vaguely remembered him telling me that all his tools and materials were kept in the toolshed outside, when he'd shown me round the house. Now, I hurried there, hoping he wouldn't see me. The coast was clear—he must have been mending a fence somewhere on the farm's boundary again.

The door to the toolshed seemed a bit stiff and I had to give it a good tug to get it open. My injured shoulder protested. I wandered inside and looked around for the glue. There was no Superglue, which had been my preferred type, but there was something called Crazy Glue which looked like it might be similar. It was on a shelf at the back, and I reached over the lawnmower to get to it. As I did, a gust of strong wind blew the door and it slammed. Before I could go to the door, balanced as I was over the lawnmower, it got worse. From outside, I heard a clunking noise as the one-sided latch fell into place. I looked up in surprise, thinking maybe this was a practical joke. Shaking, rattling, kicking the door, I realized I was trapped in here. It was quite dark in the shed with the door closed and I couldn't see any hinges on this side to unscrew. I tried shouldering it open but I wasn't exactly a prize bodybuilder, so it was well and truly stuck. I thought about what to do.

My phone was in my pocket. If I called Nate, he'd want to know what I was doing in here. I'd have to tell him about the ornament before I'd had a chance to fix it (if I fixed it, I was hoping he'd never notice I'd broken it).

I hesitated over calling him for fifteen minutes. What was I expecting to happen? Was I waiting for another gust of wind to rescue me? I was being ridiculous. Telling him I'd managed to get stuck in a shed was going to be fairly embarrassing. Informing him about the damaged ornament was even worse. On the other hand, I could just sit in here and wait for… what? No, I had to get out of the shed, there was no alternative.

Taking a deep breath, feeling like a complete prat, I pulled out my phone and rang Nate.

"Hi, Nate, it's Izzy. So… I'm stuck in the toolshed," I began.

He burst out laughing. I had to admit, it was quite funny.

"How d'you get stuck in the toolshed?" he asked.

"The wind blew the door shut. Look, is there any chance you could let me out, please? I think one of the spiders is eyeing me up," I asked.

"Sure, I'll be there once I've fixed this fence. Hang tight, pretty lady, I'll be with you when I can," he said.

"Thank you!" I said, trying to stay breezy.

I hoped that had sounded casual. I didn't want him thinking I couldn't handle being trapped in a toolshed. I mean, aside from the fact that I was depending on him to rescue me.

• • • • • • •

When Isabel called me, I was up a ladder in the middle of putting up some new fence posts. If it wasn't goat-proof, we'd lose our milk source. She wasn't in any immediate danger in the toolshed and, while I felt bad about leaving her there, the fence posts could come down if I didn't get them fixed properly.

That would set me back three hours of work. I got on with what I was doing. Miss Sutton would have to wait. I pictured her, stuck in the toolshed amongst all the hardware, in one of her delicate floral dresses and her neat shoes.

She was a fair distraction, and I near hit my thumb with the rubber mallet as I hammered home this post, driving it into the ground with brute force. She had sounded fairly buoyant on the phone. Another half hour or so wouldn't harm her, I hoped. I wondered what she'd been doing in there in the first place. If I'd had any inkling that she was going to go to the toolshed today, I would've warned her about that door.

She called me again while I was fixing the last staple into the last post to hold the wire in place. I couldn't reach my phone so I concentrated on what I was doing.

Taking a step back, I admired my handiwork. That would keep its shape. I gathered up the tools and supplies that were left over and headed back to the shed to release the young lady.

When I opened the door, she launched herself at me like a little indignant tigress.

"You left me in the shed! Anything could have happened to me in there! I've a bloody good mind to serve you dry salad for lunch!" she declared, gesturing madly.

I took hold of her arms and held them firmly in place. She seemed to melt at my touch.

"Were you hurt?" I asked her.

"No, but that's not the point," she fumed.

"Were you in immediate need of help?" I asked.

"Yes. I'd already held off calling you for fifteen minutes because I was so embarrassed. What kind of an idiot gets stuck in a shed like that? And anyway—" She seemed to cut off the next thing she wanted to say.

"Well, I see no reason why I should have known that, young lady. And if you don't stop sassing me I'm going to have to put you over my knee. Since the woodshed's right next door and all," I said, hoping to lift her indignance a little and get her to come out with whatever it was she wasn't saying.

"Anyway, I wanted to get out of there straight away so I could fix the ornament I broke before you saw it…" She stopped talking and bit her lip.

I had to laugh.

"Is that why you were in the toolshed?" I asked.

She nodded, looking up at me with round emerald eyes.

"I didn't want you to find out until I'd fixed it. I'm sorry," she said.

"How did it get broken?" I asked gently.

"I … um… was dancing around the… around the living room. Then I couldn't reach the mantel… so I… um… grabbed a chair and tried to jump on it," she said in a small voice. "But I sort of missed and I fell off."

"Did you hurt yourself?" I asked after thinking for a moment about the best way to handle this; I was glad she was enjoying herself enough to be dancing while she worked, but at the same time I was not remotely happy that she'd put herself in danger like that.

"I just bumped my shoulder on the stonework," she said. "It's fine now."

"Why don't you show me the broken ornament, and we'll see if we can fix it together?" I didn't really care about the stupid ornament but I had to get her out of the toolshed somehow so I could investigate this injury she was pooh-poohing.

She nodded, still gripping the glue, and walked me back to the house, where she showed me the little sheet of newspaper on the kitchen table. My heart sank. One of the bluebirds from the mantelpiece was in pieces.

"That was high above the stone fireplace before it fell," I said quietly.

"I'm sorry, I didn't do it on purpose. I wanted to fix it so you'd never even tell."

"I know you didn't do it on purpose, Miss Sutton, but you did still damage something that was precious to me, because you were being careless," I said. Of course, the precious thing I was worried about was her, not the ornament. Why hadn't she used a stepladder?

"I didn't know," she said. Suddenly, I got the strong feeling she was trying to minimize the whole incident.

"Let me see your shoulder, please." I was willing to bet that she was downplaying her injury, too. Sure enough, when she unbuttoned her top and showed me her shoulder, there was an angry red bump on it. It needed ice.

"That could have been your head," I said quietly. The idea that she might, right now, be bleeding out on the carpet while I was outside fixing a fence was too much to bear. I tried to keep my emotions under control and walked to the freezer and pulled out a bag of frozen peas. I wrapped it in an apron because there was nothing else within reaching distance, and I returned to the living room.

"Press this to your shoulder." I handed it to her.

She winced when she first touched it to the injury, but the look of sheer relief on her face when the coldness reached the right place told me all I needed to know about how much pain she was in.

"Miss Sutton, please show me your tasks," I added. She pulled out the paper with her free hand and gave it to me.

"What does it say next to dusting?" I asked.

"Carefully. With a stepladder," she replied.

"Did you dust carefully?" I asked.

"No."

"And you didn't use a stepladder either, did you?"

She shook her head. Judging by the color her face became, I think that's when she realized that it wasn't quite as much of an accident as she'd thought.

"I am terribly sorry about the ornament. How can I make it up to you?" she asked.

Her face melted my heart and I just wanted to kiss her. But she had not taken due care with her work and as a result she had put herself in danger.

I put the bird down and took her hands, so she would

50

know I was worried about her safety rather than the bluebird.

"I am disappointed that you ignored the instruction I wrote on your list of tasks, but more than anything, I'm concerned that you hurt yourself because of your behavior. It could have been so much worse, and I want you to be safe. If you want to make it right, you're going to have to ask me for a spanking, to square things up between us," I said.

She looked horrified.

"I have to—to ask?"

"I won't accept anything less," I replied. She looked like a rabbit caught in the headlights.

"Um…" She shook her head and looked up at me plaintively.

"You have to ask by sunset tonight—and not in front of the boys, d'you hear me?" I said.

She nodded.

"Good girl. I'm sure you'll figure it out," I said, and left her to get back on with my work. At this rate, I wouldn't be done with my fences before sunset. At least that would give her shoulder time to calm down now that she'd gotten some ice on it.

When I looked back over my shoulder, I saw her standing in the kitchen window in a slight daze.

• • • • • • •

Walking away from the house, I saw him pause and look back, then he carried on. I got a good view of his amazingly toned arse and strong shoulders. He emerged from the toolshed with some more fencing materials as I watched his muscles work, until he was out of sight, mending more fences.

Of course, now I had a fence to mend. I had to ask him for a spanking.

For the rest of the day, my thoughts were on a carousel,

going round and round, never stopping.

How could I ask him for a spanking? What words should I use? Would it hurt as much this time? Would he hold me again, afterwards, and tell me everything was all right? What had I gotten myself into?

So many questions, but really as the day wore on I saw that they boiled down to one simple one: What did I want? My instinct was to make everything right and settle things between us. Was there anything more than that? I had to admit that I had read the instruction to dust carefully, and to use a stepladder, and I had probably never dusted in my life with less care than I did today.

I wanted him to approve of me. And I wasn't sure that he did. Sometimes it seemed like we were getting on really well, and other times I felt like I had struck a nerve.

If only I could know whether he liked me. He must have noticed how turned on I got after he spanked me before. I wasn't going to put myself out there to discover that this was one-sided. What a terribly embarrassing thing to do.

Did that affect whether I should ask him for a spanking? Probably not.

I knew what I had to do, but admitting that I had done wrong, and that I craved a spanking—maybe even needed a spanking—to make me feel like everything was right between us, it was more than I could stand to do.

At the same time, I didn't know why it was so hard. Nate clearly got something out of all this, otherwise why would he do it? My shoulder calmed until I couldn't notice it as the day went on. The ice had definitely helped. Why hadn't I thought of that? I had been so worried about fixing his broken bluebird I'd ignored my own injury.

Just as I was about to serve dinner, when the boys were playing on the porch, Nate entered the kitchen. I could feel his presence behind me before he said a word.

"Have you got anything you want to say to me yet?" he prompted. I stood still, not turning to look at him. I didn't want him to see my face.

"I—um, well…" I floundered, colored red, and struggled to hold onto the plate I'd just picked up.

"Never mind, I'll ask again later," he said, and went out to see the boys.

How did he render me tongue-tied like that?

In the end, it wasn't until long after I'd put the boys to bed and lain in my own bed struggling to get the courage together that I finally managed to see him. Good thing it was summer and the sun hadn't set yet.

Leaving my bed, I crept to his room. I took a deep breath and tapped on his door.

"Yeah?" He held the door open a crack so I could only see his face.

"Can… can I come in, please?" I asked.

"Sure." He held the door for me and I stepped inside.

His room was larger than mine, and had a wardrobe at one side and a large double bed against one wall, with small bedside tables either side. He closed the door behind me then sat on the end of the bed. I looked at him hopefully, willing him to just tell me I needed a spanking. He grinned.

"Is there something you wanted to tell me, Miss Sutton?" he asked.

I looked pointedly at the floor, but I could feel his gaze on me, so I closed my eyes.

"Please, can you spank me?" I asked.

"I'm proud of you for asking. Of course I can," he said amiably. "Let me see your shoulder first though. I want to make sure you're fit to take this."

I showed him again, half hoping he'd decide he couldn't spank me after all, but half-hoping he'd see that I was okay, that he'd maybe go easier on me because my behavior hadn't caused me to be *that* badly hurt.

"It's looking a lot better than when I first saw it. Swelling's gone right down. Is it still hurting you?"

"No," I said truthfully. Whenever I bruised, it always seemed to hurt an unbelievable amount when it first happened, then after a couple of hours it would fade to nothing—unless I hit the same spot again.

"I think we're good to go then. Now I don't want my boys being wakened, so while you were making dinner I got us a little place set up. Get some shoes on and follow me please, young lady."

He led me down the stairs and out of the back door. Past the toolshed and the barn, and into the woodshed.

He held the door for me. A light came on and he closed the door behind him.

"Since you seem to like a good shed, I thought you might appreciate the surroundings," he said, grinning. The meaning was slightly lost on me. There was a wooden chair facing the middle of the room, next to a workbench. The rest of the shed was filled with logs of wood. The smell of freshly cut wood had always been one of my favorites, and now it relaxed me. I'd done the hardest part, I'd asked for my spanking, and now I just had to go through with it. It was going to hurt, but afterwards I would feel better. He sat down on the wooden chair and looked straight into my eyes.

"You'd better get yourself over my knee, young lady," he said in a stern voice, and I didn't dare disobey.

I nodded and shuffled forward, then he took my hand and gently but surely pulled me over his knee. I felt like I belonged there, like it was what I was trying to find on those nights when I was lying in bed unable to sleep. Through my fluffy dressing gown, he rubbed his hand over my bottom and I purred.

"Can you please tell me why you're about to get spanked?" he prompted.

"Because I was careless after being told to take special care with the dusting, and I broke one of your ornaments, and did something dangerous, and I wasn't planning on telling you unless you found out,"

"That's right," he said, and then he turned up my dressing gown and paused for a moment.

"Miss Sutton," he said. "Am I to take it that you came to my room with no nightwear on underneath your robe, or underwear besides?"

I nodded.

"That hardly seems appropriate for a young lady meeting with her employer to rectify a mistake that put her in danger, now, does it?" he asked. "I could get quite the wrong idea about you."

"I'm sorry, Mr. Byrne," I said, not quite sure whether he was joking or being serious. He trailed his fingers over my skin.

"I was going to warm up with spanking you over your panties, but since you aren't wearing any, I will have to start on your bare bottom. I'm not going to go any easier on you on account of that," he said, and brought his hand down on my left cheek.

The sting was sharp and I was reminded of how much the first spanking had hurt. As he continued to spank me, I wiggled my bottom and kicked my legs to try to quell the burn. He was spanking much harder here, and I could feel his arousal under my hip. After several minutes, he stopped. I wasn't crying yet. I was certain it wasn't over.

"Now I'm going to apply this lovely piece of wood to your naughty bottom," he said, showing it to me. My eyes widened in horror. Contrary to the last, my nether regions betrayed me again. I was dripping wet, and it seemed I wasn't the only one.

I could taste his arousal in the air around us, mingling with the fresh pine scent of the woodshed.

Wasting no time, he brought the wood down right on my sit spot.

I yelped and kicked.

The wood was definitely worse than the belt—it was so inflexible and big!

He continued to apply it to my bottom and very soon I was crying. It felt so solid when it connected with my bum. As he continued, I found myself becoming still; lost in the moment, accepting my fate. If you'd touched the fire in my backside at that moment, you probably would have burned your fingers. Tears rolled quietly up my forehead and dripped onto the floor. He was right, of course. Damn him, he was *always* right. That *could* have been my head that got injured, and I might be in hospital right now trying to remember my own name. Why hadn't I just dusted sensibly?

"Last three," he said. "You're nearly there."

I counted them in my head and cried even more once it was over. He rubbed my sore bottom and made it hurt less, all the while holding me with his other hand.

"Shh, shh, it's all right, it's all right. You did well. It's all over now. All is forgiven. Just don't do it again, Miss Sutton," he said, soothing me. I cried myself out, and just stayed there, over his knee, exhausted, tearful, but feeling better at the same time.

"I'm so sorry," I tried to say, but it came out garbled. He just kept soothing me. I think he knew what I meant to say.

"Shh, it's okay," he reiterated.

While I was in a slight reverie, he covered my bottom with my soft dressing gown—making me wince slightly—then took me in his arms and carried me back to the house and upstairs. He laid me down on his bed and climbed in beside me. Under the covers, he wrapped his arms around me. I'd never felt so safe, so loved, so protected. I wanted him to take me, here, hard, but at the same time I just wanted to stay cuddled up with him.

"Are you okay?" he asked.

I nodded drowsily. I fell asleep in his arms, and I'd never slept so well in my life before. This was where I belonged. I didn't dream, I just slept, at peace and relaxed.

CHAPTER SIX

I opened my eyes. This room was unfamiliar. Where had I fallen asleep last night? It transpired that I was in Nate's bed as I looked over at him. He was awake.

"Morning, Sleeping Beauty," he said, that grin on his face again.

Oh. My. God.

I was absolutely positive that all we'd done was fallen asleep on the same bed, but it was still too far, wasn't it? I mean, in all honesty the *spankings* were probably too far but this really pushed the envelope. I leapt out of bed and searched for my dressing gown. The boys couldn't see this. I found my dressing gown and fastened it tightly with a double knot then ran out to my own room, where I sat on my bed with my head in my hands.

Well done, silly girl, you've probably just made him think that you don't like him.

My response was reasonable! I countered.

No, your response was typical, *there's a difference.*

My logical rational thoughts were being confrontational this morning. Were they right?

I knew I was getting caught up over him. In what universe could I ever allow this to continue?

I had no wish to be forward with my employer, and that's exactly who Nate was. My employer. I had no business being in his bed no matter how tempting the thought might be. Not only that, but I had no intention to stay here after the summer was over. It seemed singularly unfair to let Nate know that I liked him—perhaps even loved him—then to have to extricate myself, regardless of my feelings, when the term commenced once again and I returned to Berkeley. Even if we survived the fourteen-hour round trip to see each other for the next twelve months, I had to go back to the UK after my next student visa expired. I had seen the entry requirements for a green card; I knew I didn't meet them. I didn't know if our relationship would last even if we were in the same physical location—what hope did we have if we were separated by an ocean?

What if, instead of a desk job, I managed to land a coveted contract as a field research assistant, or similar? I could end up anywhere in the world, living with members of the Maasai tribe in Africa, or observing indigenous Russians in the eight hundred mile reservation east of Magadan; I might even be tasked with examining a western culture in a warm climate such as sunny Spain. And that was only if I didn't go straight for a PhD. I'd always wanted to be Doctor Isabel Sutton. It had a nice ring to it. I'd have to be willing and ready to travel to wherever the best doctoral supervisor worked, as well as wherever my research took me. The point was, I had options and ideas, and I wanted to do all of these things and more.

I had sworn to myself that I would never let a relationship get in the way of my plans to travel and have a career. Relationships didn't last, careers did. I couldn't—no, I wouldn't—let this potential relationship get in the way of my lifelong dreams.

That was what I thought when I thought about it with my head. However, my heart longed for just one more caress of his hand on my bare, freshly spanked skin, and my nether regions agreed.

What was I to do?

I had to carry on as if nothing had happened.

Pulling myself together, I went downstairs and prepared breakfast—toast for everyone, since I baked bread the previous day.

Nate walked into the kitchen and sent my thoughts swirling again. His mere presence was enough to make me gush. I was definitely aroused by his strength, his reassuring demeanor, and the way he just always knew what to do in any given situation.

I excused myself and went to fetch the boys, but as I passed him he grabbed my wrist.

"We need to talk, young lady."

I tried not to swoon at the way he used his *young lady* voice, as if I were an incorrigible charge and he were left with no other choice but to take me in hand.

"Please, Nate. Their toast is ready," I pleaded with him. He let it drop and I escaped to wake the children.

Watching him eat his toast, the slices dwarfed in his hands, his manly thick fingers perched on the crusts, was more than I could bear, and I tried to focus my attention on Mason and Taylor, who were spreading strawberry jam on their plates.

"You boys better eat that jelly," Nate said.

"I'm going to dip my bread, and Mason's copying me," Taylor said.

"No, I'm not. You're copying me," Mason replied.

"You're both going to dip your bread now that you've covered your plates in jelly, and that's the end of it," Nate said with a firm-but-kind manner. The boys did as they were told.

When he was around the boys, I saw his tender, paternal side, which just made me love him more.

After breakfast, he cornered me.

"Taylor, Mason, why don't you run along now and play outside," Nate said, using a firm tone that made it clear it wasn't really a suggestion.

They went out and I was alone with Nate, with no reason not to speak to him.

• • • • • • •

She had been acting weird all morning; it was like she didn't want to talk about the previous night. I sent the boys out and tried to get her attention but she busied herself with washing the dishes. I stood beside her.

"Isabel Sutton, I intend to talk to you about last night," I said, trying to be very clear.

She spun around and looked at me with anguished eyes, then dropped the towel and fled upstairs.

I sighed.

Why couldn't she just talk to me about it? I was trying to make it as easy as possible for her.

I felt like I'd caught a timid little bird in my cupped hands. I could feel her flittering her wings against my fingers, looking in every direction, unable to settle. It seemed reasonable from the bird's point of view, although I knew she had nothing to be afraid of with me. If only she would stop wasting so much energy flapping her wings.

I went upstairs and knocked on her door, hoping I could talk some sense into her. When she didn't answer, I tried the handle. Unusually for her, she hadn't locked it. Did that mean she wanted me to go in? I wished I spoke the language of little flitter birds.

I opened the door and went in.

Under the covers, a small figure lay with her face in the pillow; all I could see was a cascade of auburn hair. I perched on the end of the bed.

"This is the opposite of talking, Miss Sutton," I said.

"Wstfgl," came the reply.

"I can't hear you with your head buried in the pillow," I said. "Tell me what's going on."

She shook her head.

"I can't help you if you don't talk to me." I wasn't going

anywhere. She shook her head again.

"Isabel Sutton, get your head out of that pillow and talk to me right now or I'll spank that bottom until it turns purple."

Under her lovely hair, her shoulders started to shake. Not wanting to startle her, I settled for stroking her right calf through the sheet. I was willing to bet she would start talking when she stopped crying.

"I can't be with you," she said after several minutes.

"What do you mean, you can't be with me?" I asked. We were together now.

"I... I feel something for you," she said. "Only I can't. You're my employer." She started crying again. "And I don't want to leave. Because then I would miss you."

I just started to laugh.

"Is that what's got you all riled up?" I asked her. "You want to leave because you're getting too attached but you're too attached to leave? Is that the gist of it?"

"That is, in fact, about the long and short of it," she nodded.

I sighed and shook my head.

"Look, Isabel, if our relationship—if that's what this is turning into—is going somewhere, I know that between us we will find a way to compromise," I said gently. "If it's meant to be, we'll make it work out somehow. As a team. But you aren't the only person involved here, and it's not right for you to bottle up your feelings like this and not let me be involved in decision making when it directly affects me. I like to think that while I'm a take-charge sort of man, at the same time I give you a fair opportunity to share your opinion. If you'll share it. We fell asleep in the same bed; it's not like we woke up married to each other. Why, Miss Sutton, I ought to spank you for getting bent out of shape over something so small without even talking to me first," I finished with a grin.

That cheered her up. One of the things I liked about Isabel was that she got my sense of humor.

She sat up, wiping away the tears, with a warm smile.

"I'd better get back to… um… whatever it was I was doing before *somebody* decided to ask twenty questions," she said, standing up. I got off the bed and caught her hand before she ran off again.

"Wait." I said.

I stepped forward, leaned in so close I could smell her fruity shampoo, I tucked her fluffy red hair behind her ears with my hands so I had a clear view of her face. I looked into her emerald eyes and kissed her passionately. She yielded her mouth to me, letting me plunder it with my tongue, explore her from the inside, while she made little happy noises. Her kiss tasted like sweet chocolate.

After several seconds, we broke apart.

"You can stop by my room later tonight and make up for it," I said in a husky voice. Not that there was anything to make up for, of course, and I could tell that she knew I wasn't serious. The look she gave me… I thought she was going to melt into my own personal puddle of Isabel, right there on her bedroom floor. Then, before my eyes, I watched her gather her wits from where I'd just scattered them. I clapped her gently on the bottom as she skipped past me.

"Eight thirty, I'll be waiting for you. Don't be late, young lady," I said, remaining where I was.

The hardness in my pants needed time to subside, or I was liable to take a tumble down the stairs.

I'd never got even the slightest hint of a boner from kissing a girl before. Something about Isabel filled me with the urge to claim her, protect her, keep her somewhere suitable for the most precious jewels, make her scream under my touch over and over again. Nothing bad would ever happen to Isabel Sutton. Not while I was around.

I went out to change the oil on my truck; it was a nice, relaxing job that I'd done so often I didn't need to concentrate too hard. That was good; I needed time to ease myself into the day. That girl had gotten inside my head and

I just had to have her.

I had to make her mine.

She seemed to feel the same way—that she wanted to be mine—but she had a few things there that she needed to work out. I could tell there was something else. Why she wasn't telling me was anybody's guess, but she was a smart girl, probably the smartest I'd ever met, so I was hoping it would work its way out with time.

· · · · · · ·

While I was waiting for Isabel, I thought it was times like this when it'd be real great if I was a big reader. Sitting on my bed doing nothing, I couldn't stop thinking about her. Still, it was twenty-five after eight, so I was sure she'd be here soon. I knew I'd come up early—heck, I'd been here since quarter past—but I couldn't exactly tell a girl 'I'll be waiting' then follow her up the stairs.

Following her up the stairs could happen later, so I could get a glimpse of that sweet ass of hers.

I stared at the ceiling and thought about her, willing the sun to go down that little bit faster, bringing in the night, and moving time on to when I'd see Isabel.

At eight thirty, my heartrate quickened and all my senses seemed heightened in anticipation. I sat up and stared at the door, waiting for her to knock on it.

…And waited. Where was she? It was now twenty to nine. It's not even like we lived in different houses; her room was only over the hallway. Oh, I'd spank her good when I got my hands on her. Little minx was probably leaving it to the last possible minute.

At quarter to nine, bitterly disappointed, I decided that she wasn't coming. I got up and opened my door to see if she was on her way. Her door was closed, and in the gap between the carpet and door, there was no light.

Sure looked like she'd gone to bed, so I closed my own door in disbelief. She'd seemed so sure this morning after our conversation. Determined not to show that she'd hurt me, I wouldn't pressure her about it. I was going to come out of this with my dignity intact if not my heart.

Frustrated and confused, I sat on the bed. The day had been exhausting, and to top it off, being stood up in my own home? It was time for sleep; I could deal with this tomorrow. The light snapped off and I got under the covers.

A few minutes later, I heard a gentle knock at the door. I had a good mind to ignore it, but some part of me that I couldn't control got up and opened it.

"I—I'm sorry. I fell asleep about an hour ago, and just woke up. Am I too late?" she asked.

Her voice, her smell… the sight of her in her soft robe, lost under its bulk… I couldn't deny how I felt about her. Her emerald eyes were so bright and hopeful.

"Come on in," I said, holding the door for her.

She shuffled in and I closed it behind her then rearranged the sheets, which had gotten screwed up when I went for the door.

I sat on the bed; she perched awkwardly. For a few seconds neither of us said anything.

"Why do I feel like you're still confused about things, Miss Sutton?" I asked her.

She looked uncomfortable for a second, thinking about something she didn't like, then she returned to her usual self again, and it was like the sun had come out from behind a cloud.

"It's nothing," she said. I nodded. She wasn't ready to talk about it. I'd let her get to telling me about it in her own time, unless she started acting like she did this morning again. When she was that stressed, she clearly needed to come out with what was bothering her.

"I tell you what, Miss Sutton, why don't you tell me how you'd decorate the interior if you could have your own yacht?" I suggested, reverting to something we both had in common. I hoped I might find out more about her likes and dislikes, see where we'd got some common ground. We were very different in a lot of ways, but I thought that was a good thing. After all, who wanted to date themselves? Not me, that's for sure.

"I'd paint the whole inside a beautiful pale sea green… is aquamarine a real color?" she asked.

"If you can think it up, someone can mix it," I assured her. It was a nice color, but if it was the same color as the sea, wouldn't it get boring after a while? I'd prefer a nice dark red, classy, like a nice wine. One of those colors with names like Bordeaux or Merlot. Wait, weren't we fantasizing about our own separate yachts? I thought about having Isabel on my dream yacht… she fit into the mental image quite nicely, I was surprised to notice.

"Yeah, aquamarine then. Then I'd put in portholes; I know some boats have those rectangular windows these days but I guess I'm an old-fashioned girl at heart and I'd want round windows," she continued.

"Portholes… that's a great idea," I said. "I always wanted them on a boat too. I wonder why they call them that."

"No idea," she replied. "Anyway, then I'd probably want a nice bathroom—only it'd be a shower, sink, and toilet, no bath. The idea of a bath full of water inside a boat floating at sea just seems too mind-boggling to me," she said with a little giggle.

"What about a sit bath?" I asked. "They're easier to install than a shower tray, or so I hear."

"Ugh, God, no! We had one of those in a caravan in Skegness, the only year we had a staycation. Those bloody things are utterly miserable. The worst of both worlds!" she said dismissively. "But I'd definitely want a hammock, they look so much fun, maybe a double hammock—do they make those?"

She looked so beautiful when she talked animatedly about something she'd really thought about, and I could see that nobody and nothing would ever get between her and her dreams.

"They sure do," I said.

She carried on describing her ideal yacht, and I thought her ideas said a lot about her; for example, she wanted a bookshelf just below the ceiling, for all her favorite books. It hadn't occurred to me to take books (except the engine's manual), but it would be useful to have a few others. I liked the occasional story but I wasn't really a bookworm. Then there was her other storage idea.

"So where the staircase is, take all the steps off—the bits you stand on—and make them into little cupboards, where you can store small items, freeing up space elsewhere for larger things," she explained.

"Then how would you use the stairs?" I asked.

"Silly! You put hinges on the steps—just at the back—then put them back where they started, so you lift each of them up to get at the storage under them," she said. I laughed.

"If I ever get a yacht, you're going to make me one of those staircases," I said.

She looked wistful for a moment.

"Do you think you will? Get a yacht, I mean?" she asked.

"I hope so," I said. "It's been my dream for a while; I guess I'm just waiting for the right time to do it."

The conversation turned to more mundane subjects, then Isabel yawned.

"That's your bedtime, young lady," I said.

She looked sad at the prospect of having to leave.

"Come here." I pulled the top sheet back and patted the mattress. Surprised, she got in and I turned the light off then joined her.

That fruity smell of her hair was delectable. I stroked it wistfully, savoring the softness.

One day soon, I intended to take her, hard, truly make her mine, and curl up with her like this afterwards. For tonight, however, I was just glad to have such a pretty girl in my bed. I put my arm around her and waited for her breathing to settle, telling me she was asleep, before I reluctantly closed my own eyes and slept.

•••••••

I was icing a cake to go with dinner when Nate crashed into the kitchen looking like he'd just won the lottery.

"Isabel, the goats are kidding!" he cried. "Come and help!"

"What do you mean, they're kidding?" I asked. They'd started a comedy act? He'd used the word before but the meaning didn't quite register this time.

"They're giving birth!" he said.

"Lambing?" I asked.

"Goats don't birth lambs. C'mon!" He seemed very impatient to get back out to them.

I put the spatula down—the icing wouldn't go off—and hurried outside with him.

In the goat shed, two goats were indeed standing awkwardly, in labor.

"Do they usually do it at the same time?" I asked incredulously.

"No! Usually they're a few days apart if they conceived at the same time. This has never happened before and I'm going to need help getting these delivered."

"When you say help…" I put my hands up in front of me and took a step backwards. "I'm not going to have to stick my arm up there, am I?" I'd seen *Countryfile* enough times to be worried about this.

"Depends what the problem is. Now, I'm not a goat expert—I just keep 'em—but the only thing I can think of that would require you to do that would be if it was breach and we couldn't get the vet out," Nate said. "That's the first thing you can do to help; watch the goats for me while I call a vet and give them a heads up that we might be needing them later."

I nodded, more confidently than I felt, and Nate left me on my own with the two goats. What was I watching them for? Would I know if I saw it? What was I supposed to do if anything happened? I really had no idea what I was doing, and I was so scared of messing this up.

I tentatively put out a hand and patted one of the goats on the nose.

"There, there," I said, but it came out flat and sarcastic. Her nose was so soft. She moved her nose to sniff my hand, then opened her mouth. Just in time I remembered that goats will try to eat anything that's not a part of themselves, and I pulled my hand back. She looked at me warily; every goat I've ever met always seem to be planning something.

We stood, staring each other out, sizing each other up, for several minutes. At my uncle's smallholding back home, they'd kept sheep, which were much more docile and easygoing than these two slightly scary goats. When I'd patted a sheep on the head, it had at least got the common courtesy to look reassured.

I was still at loggerheads with the goat when Nate returned.

"Vet's been warned, he'll come out if it gets sticky. I need to let him know when we're not likely to need him any more so he can go to bed."

"But it's only half ten in the morning!" I said. "Do you really think they'll take that long?"

"Could do," Nate replied. "Why don't you go get us a big pail of hot water and some cloths from the utility room?"

"How hot?" I asked.

"Hot enough to stay warm; we're going to need it to clean up when the kids arrive. You won't want to touch the taps when you're covered in goat though."

I ran to fetch the hot water, filled a pail from the kitchen taps then hefted it back to the goat shed.

We covered the area around the goats in empty feed bags as Nate said they were easy to throw away once they were messy, and we gently prepared the goats, ready to assist with the delivery, although really they were doing most of it by themselves.

Glinda, the goat who had been staring me out earlier, was closer to crowning than the other goat. When the kids emerged, I felt privileged to be watching these new lives come into the world. I'd seen *lambing* before, of course, but that didn't make it any less special. She had her two kids easily and seemed to be saying, 'I do this all the time. Now where's the food?' We pretty much just had to clean the kids off with paper towels, dip their umbilical cords in iodine, and they were fine. Elphie, however, had problems.

"Glinda's washing her newborns. She can be left to bond with them for a little while—we still need to see her feed them, but she doesn't need our full attention," Nate explained. "Elphie needs our care more right now."

"What's wrong with her?" I asked as she tried to lie down again. Every time her swollen stomach touched the floor, she bleated and stood back up again.

"I can see the bubble but it's hard to make out what the problem is. Pass me a flashlight, would you?" Nate said.

I handed him the light and watched in amazement as he shone it, looking around for signs of what was wrong with the goat.

"There's too many legs," he said. "They're supposed to come out one at a time, and these kids are all tangled up."

"What can we do about it?" I asked.

"I'm going to have to try to disentangle them, see if I can get them to wait their turn," he said amiably. I giggled, but I was also a little bit worried. Would Elphie be okay?

"Rather you than I," I said.

"Just hold the flashlight for me. I'm going in," he said.

After everything I imagined he'd seen and done in the army, let alone the fact that he'd obviously done this before on his farm, I suppose he didn't get squeamish about things like this. I, on the other hand, couldn't stand to watch. When the delivery had been trouble-free, with Glinda, I'd been unable to look away; it was fascinating. This, however, was making me cringe somewhat and I was trying very hard not to show it.

I held the flashlight and stared at a point just above the goat's raised tail.

"You're doing fine, Isabel," Nate said, and I felt a little reassured. "If it's too much, I'll get the boys to help out instead."

Wait. The children could manage this? They'd been here for a birth? Mind you, boys that age were all about disgusting things. Not for nothing did the saying go that boys were made of slugs and snails and puppy dog tails.

"No, no, it's no trouble at all," I said, sounding more confident than I felt.

I continued to do my best to assist while Nate did the hard job of sorting out which legs belonged to whom, all the while poor Elphie was utterly confused and kept trying to push. Eventually, however, the first baby goat came tumbling out and landed on some of the feed bags. I cut and cleaned the cord then put the kid before his mother. She started licking him at once, seeming to welcome the distraction from what was going on behind her.

"We have number two!" Nate cried, and the second goat emerged, looking very dazed. I wanted to jump for joy but of course we were not out of the woods yet—there was another kid inside her that needed to come out.

"I think the third one's in distress. It hasn't moved after the first two came out," Nate said. He reached in again and seemed to be attempting to pull one leg then another, although it was difficult for me to see what he was doing from where I had returned to shine the flashlight.

"Oh, this is real bad. I can't get a hold of the last baby goat—he's too far back. The umbilical cord's stuck around the kid's neck. We gotta get him out fast," Nate said. "My hands are too big… I'm sorry, Isabel, but we're going to lose the third kid unless you can get it out."

I blanched. Feeling more terrified of getting this wrong than of the mess, I stepped forward nervously and handed Nate the flashlight. This baby goat's life was in my hands?

Was I going to be able to live up to the trust Nate was placing in me? I knelt down, closed my eyes, and put my hand in, but the rubber gloves I was wearing were stopping me from being able to really feel what I was doing.

"There are two legs in front of you. You need to ease one through the opening, then the other, and keep switching which leg you're pulling, so the baby goat just comes out gently," Nate said. I started to shake with stress as I tried to follow his instructions.

Nate laid a comforting elbow on my shoulder; his hands were still in the rubber gloves.

"You are doing just fine, Isabel, don't think about it too much," Nate said, and I felt reassured that he was here to guide me through this. "That's it, gently does it, you're nearly there."

"I'm so scared," I quavered, trying to get my hand to steady.

"Trust *me*, Isabel, if you don't trust yourself. I wouldn't have asked you to help if I didn't think you could do it," There was a beautiful moment when I believed him. I wiggled the goat's forelegs until it was crowning, then everything seemed to speed up and the goat was out, we cut off the umbilical cord and unfastened it from the poor kid's neck, and Nate gave it a gentle slap to get it breathing again. The mother urged the other two kids to feed, nuzzling them toward her teats with her nose, then she took to washing her third baby. We cleaned up the floor by just rolling up the feed bags we'd put down, then both of us slumped on the floor, absolutely filthy, but able to breathe normally again.

"That was bloody tense," I declared.

"You did a swell job. Look, Isabel, see that third kid? He's alive because of you," Nate said, removing his gloves.

The enormity of what we'd just done filled me with tears and I tried to hold them back. If I started crying now I wasn't sure I'd be able to stop.

"I'm so proud of you," Nate said, and that was it, I was

sobbing on the floor of the goat shed. He put his arms around me and rubbed my back, soothing me, kissing me on the forehead. "You did so well," he said. "You really did. It's all okay now." I let him hold me until I'd cried myself out, then slowly I sat up.

"I could sure use a shower," Nate said.

"Same here," I replied. He stared at me in confusion. "It means 'me too.'" I added.

"Let's get these clothes in the wash, then you and I should go take a very, very long shower," he grinned suggestively. I liked the idea of doing something stress-relieving around about now.

We checked in on Glinda, who was now happily feeding her two kids at the same time, then left our new mother goats to be with their kids, as they seemed to know what they were doing, and we went inside.

It was going dark, and Taylor and Mason were sitting in the living room watching TV with the volume very high.

"When's dinner, dad?" Mason asked above the noise of cartoon spaceships shooting lasers at each other. He was always thinking with his stomach.

"Soon as Miss Sutton and I have cleaned off. We got five new baby goats!" Nate replied.

"Cool! Can we see them?" Mason asked.

"Not yet, kiddo. Let them get to know their mommies first," Nate said. "We'll be back real soon then how's about we send out for pizza?"

Pacified with the prospect of fast food, the boys settled to watching TV again and Nate and I went to the bathroom. I locked the door while he turned the shower on. It was over the bath with a curtain, so we both fitted in with no bumped elbows. I picked up the shower gel and flicked it open.

"I'll do that," Nate said, and took the bottle out of my hands.

I watched him squeeze a bit of the fruity shower gel into his hands, then he put the bottle down and lathered the liquid soap up. He started with my neck, massaging the soap in underneath my hair, then down my décolleté, before taking my left breast in both of his hands and massaging the soap into the delicate skin. He traced his fingers around my areola and I gasped at the sensation. The water seemed to make his movements slicker, his hands feeling like silk as he comprehensively covered me in fruit-scented bubbles and rubbed my body until I felt clean again. When he went down one leg and back up the other, the only thing left was my pussy. He cupped it with a hand full of warm water after rinsing the suds from his hands, then let the water—and his hand—sit there for a moment while I gasped at the amazing feel of it, before he gently stroked my pussy lips and honed in on my clit, at which point I moaned softly then put my hand over my mouth. We needed to be quiet so the boys didn't hear.

He rubbed it some more. "Seems like it's not coming clean," he caught my eye and winked at me. He leaned in and lapped his tongue against it.

I shuddered at the new pleasure, something I'd never felt before, and then tried to make my legs be still while he went down on me. The idea that anyone wanted to do something just for me was potent. Very quickly, I could feel the pressure building and soon I was on the edge of an orgasm. I held onto Nate's shoulders to stop myself falling over as waves of pleasure crashed over me.

When I came back to my senses, Nate was still where he'd been, but he had stopped licking me, and now he slowly stood up. His cock had hardened and I shamelessly ogled it. I wanted it *now*. At that moment in time I didn't even care about the long-term consequences of shagging my employer. I needed him inside me like I'd never needed anything before in my life.

"Lean over and hold onto the faucets." He murmured, his voice betraying how turned on he was. I complied, and he pushed into me from behind. The feeling of his hot, wet cock sliding into me was delicious, and I gripped the taps trying to keep myself from crying out again. He started to move in and out, gently at first, but then faster strokes, his cock hitting all the right spots inside of me, making me gasp. The water hit my bottom and splashed deliciously, creating a fine mist. Just as I was getting used to the rhythm he did something completely unexpected. My eyes widened in surprise as I felt something pushing against my other opening.

"What are you doing?" I had frozen.

"Relax. Trust me. I know what I'm doing," he said.

"Nobody's ever... nothing's ever been in there." I started to get a little shrill.

"You're tensing up. Just relax, let me explore you, I'm going to make you feel real good," he breathed into my ear.

Something must have gotten through to my stressed arse muscles because they loosened enough for his finger to slide in a little way. It felt enormous; I could feel the entire shape of it inside me. Through the weird stretching feeling, and my arse trying to expel the new invader, there was an undertone of immense pleasure. I tried to hold onto that and discard the other sensations.

"That's it, let it in," he said, as if he could feel that I'd relaxed. Next thing I knew, the finger had started to move. With his cock still inside me as well, I felt very filled.

He began fucking me again with his cock and his finger, and his other hand caressed my clit making me ready to explode again any second. I could feel him getting closer to his own release as his cock went faster inside me, and soon I was riding a very intense wave. As my arse clenched down on his finger, as my pussy contracted on his cock, as his fingers stroked my clit, and I squeezed the bath taps with both hands and came. I'd never come so hard before.

Then, as I was descending from Mount Orgasm, he removed his finger, washing it off with the water, and gripped my hips. He drove into me hard until he found his own release.

Moments later, I stood up slightly stiffly and he enveloped me in a hug. We stood like that under the

74

showerhead, water streaming over us, until it started to go cold, then we turned the taps off and got out.

"It's a good thing there's plenty of towels today," I remarked as we both wrapped ourselves in fluffy towels and dried off.

"It sure is," Nate said. "C'mon, the boys will be eating each other if we don't get some food in them ASAP."

We emerged from the bathroom in towels and ran upstairs to get dressed, before returning to the living room where Taylor and Mason were still watching some loud cartoon or other, totally oblivious of what had just taken place in the bathroom.

In bed that night I still felt the afterglow. That man was a genius; how had he known exactly the right places to touch to make me come like that? I wanted him inside me all the time, filling me up, making me feel like that. It was sheer perfection.

Reality, however, encroached on my happiness. I'd just slept with my employer. And I'd liked it immensely. But the day would come when I'd have to leave and go back to the university. Oh, God, this was going to complicate things…

CHAPTER SEVEN

"Made a cloud!" Taylor declared proudly.

I looked at his blobby finger painting. Blue cloud on white sky. It was close enough.

"Well done, that's beautiful. What are you going to paint next?" I asked him.

"Truck," he said.

I wasn't sure that a truck would come out very well in the medium of finger painting, but he looked so set on the idea that I didn't have the heart to tell him. It was a four-year-old's finger painting; it wasn't like he was trying for entry to St. Marten's College, after all. If he didn't learn through experience what didn't work so well, how could he learn what did?

"I can't wait to see it," I said with a warm smile.

Mason was idly dipping his fingers in the paint and running them around the page, the multi-color version of taking a pencil line for a walk. Every time he got too close to the edge of the newspaper under the sheet of paper he was supposed to be painting on, I stopped him.

I felt an extraordinary sense of achievement today, like I'd finally got everything in the house to do what it was supposed to. I'd been here for three weeks at this point and it had all fallen into place. The washing machine was working away in the utility room, the dishes were sparkling on the drainer, and the boys were playing considerately and creatively. I felt a tad conflicted again. If this made me so happy, why was I pursuing other things? Surely if something made you happy, it was the right thing for you to do?

As I felt the return of the familiar confusion that had at least subsided for a few hours, there was a knock at the kitchen door.

"Special delivery," the postman said, but there was actually nothing requiring a signature; I think he was attempting postman humor so I smiled. "Here's your mail, lady."

"Ta very much," I said, taking the proffered post from him. He went on his way and I just stared at the top envelope.

It was addressed to me.

Me!

Who knew I was here?

I couldn't make out the postmark because it had smudged.

"You gotta open it to find out what it says." Taylor said, as if explaining the concept of a letter to someone who had never seen one before. With the face I was making, I'd probably convinced him that I *hadn't* seen a letter before.

I ripped it open and withdrew a sheet of paper.

The blood drained from my face as I read the words.

It was from Immigration.

Somehow, they'd found out I was working here. They pointed out that this was a violation of my student visa. And they wished to inform me that as a result, they were not going to renew my student visa. My current one would expire in two months.

What??

The boys were looking expectantly at me.

"Can… can you two wash your hands in the sink then go play outside on your own for a little minute? I need to, to speak to Nate—I mean your dad," I stammered. Bloody hell, I was so flustered.

"Sure we can. I'm *six*! I'll watch Taylor," Mason said in his best confidential grownup voice. He had no idea it was shattering my heart into even smaller pieces. I ran out of the kitchen to find Nate. He was in the barn, mending the hayloft.

"Hey, Isabel, could you just pass me that wrench there, please?" He waved at the wrench in question. I brought it over.

"What's the matter? Are one of the boys sick?" His face was full of concern.

I couldn't hold it in any longer. I started crying as I held the letter out to him.

He took it off me and read it.

"That's awful," he said. "Hey, hey, it's okay, come and sit down over here."

He sat on a hay bale and pulled me onto his knee.

"I can't finish my Master's," I said tearfully. "I'm going to have to go home."

"Not necessarily," he said. "I'm going to call a lawyer and see if we can't straighten this out somehow. In the meantime, young lady, you are not allowed to worry about it. We've got two months to fix this mess, and it's not over 'til it's over." He rubbed my back and I felt for all the world like everything really was going to be fine. Only I knew it wasn't.

• • • • • • •

It was an afternoon of phone calls. I called my dad and told him about Isabel's predicament. She sure was in a tight spot.

"What was the name of that immigration lawyer who helped Uncle Bernie with his wife?" I asked.

"You mean his *second* wife. He's divorced her again and now he's on number three. Brigitte from Sweden. I guess he'll be calling that lawyer again soon to get her immigration in order," he said. My dad had a very roundabout way of answering questions; I think he was finding retirement lonely, even with my mom around.

"Okay, his second wife. Who was the lawyer who sorted all that out for them?" I asked again.

"Her name was Lisa Donovan. Why? She been in the papers?" my dad asked.

"No, dad, I've… I've met a girl." I felt like I was fourteen again and bringing home my first date.

"A girl? Like… a girlfriend?" he asked.

"Yeah, something like that," I said. How did this conversation get so awkward?

"Well, I'm happy for you, son. Although, since we only live two hours away, why haven't we met her yet?" he asked.

"I've only known her for three weeks myself! Anyway, she's in a bit of hot water over some immigration problems and I'd like the number for that lawyer. Do you have it?"

"No, your Uncle Bernie never gave me the number of his lawyer because I wouldn't have cause to use it," he said. It was a reasonable observation—he'd been married to my mom since the seventies—but I wasn't in the mood for this.

"Well, could you call him for me and get it? I only met him at gramma's funeral, and I heard he was funny about answering the phone to unfamiliar numbers." I was starting to get a little exasperated with the long-windedness of this conversation.

After a stern talking-to where my dad told me I shouldn't talk back to my parents and reminded me that I was never too old to go without dessert when I next visited ("When will that be?" my mom shouted from the background), I got him to call me back with the number, which he did after a few minutes.

I called Lisa Donovan, explained the situation, then put her on speakerphone for Isabel to hear.

"Basically, you need to challenge the original decision—for example, challenge the evidence they claim proves Isabel was working. Was she working?" Lisa asked.

"She was here on my farm helping out and I gifted her a hundred dollars a week," I said carefully.

"I guess it boils down to whether you can convince them of that. If they can't produce a work contract or witnesses to say that she was at your home as a place of work, you might be able to make a case." Lisa seemed optimistic, which was reassuring.

• • • • • • •

I appreciated what Nate was doing to help, but really this was my problem and he didn't need to entangle himself in it.

The lawyer was saying something about how Immigration wouldn't want me to stay now.

"…Your issue going forward will be that the ICE will be watching you both very closely from now on, and will probably cause problems when it comes to renewing Isabel's visa in September," Lisa explained. "Second, if you don't mind me asking: Mr. Byrne and Miss Sutton, what's the nature of your relationship with one another?"

"Um…" I felt put on the spot but it was one of those now-or-never moments where I felt that if I didn't say how I felt, I might not get the chance later. I looked helplessly at Nate and neither of us said a word.

"Mr. Byrne?" Lisa prompted. She couldn't see what was going on.

"I love Isabel," he said.

My face broke out into a huge smile.

"And I love you too," I said, then the smile vanished as I realized I couldn't be with him *and* have the career I wanted, that Immigration wanted me gone, that I felt like I needed to lead two lives so everything could happen how I wanted it to, and I started crying again.

"My best advice would be for the two of you to marry one another as soon as possible—it will take a while to process a green card application," Lisa said. "Immigration will interview you both separately to assure themselves this is a genuine marriage before they leave you alone, and I suggest that, if you are going down this route, you both familiarize yourselves with every little detail about one another's family, birthdays, everything like that."

After the phone call, I continued to cry.

"What's the matter, Isabel? She said you can stay. All we have to do is get married," Nate said. I cried harder.

How could I tell him that I just wished we could have met one another in ten years' time, when I'd got my traveling out of the way and established my career the way I wanted it? I wanted to stay so badly that my heart was in agony, but I felt like I wasn't ready to be getting married and settling down when there were so many things I still wanted to do.

How could I tell him?

• • • • • • •

The phone call had been so positive, and yet here was Isabel Sutton crying her eyes out like it was the end of the world. I didn't know what had gotten into her.

"Sit down in the living room; I'm going to make you a nice cup of coffee. It'll help to take your mind off things."

"I don't want a coffee," she said.

I knew she was being stubborn and trying to not be a nuisance at the same time. That was Isabel all over. I'd bet my farm that she hadn't had a drink since breakfast, and it was now midday.

"Isabel, you're dehydrated from all that crying. You're getting a drink, young lady," I said firmly. Even drinking coffee would help a little.

She nodded.

"Yes, Nate," she said in a dead voice.

I sure hoped that coffee could cheer her up.

A few minutes later, I brought in a steaming cafetière of

fresh brewed coffee, on a tray with two mugs, since I was pretty thirsty too. I set it down on a trestle table in front of her.

"Thanks," she said.

It was like the joy had escaped from her soul.

"How's about we go down to the courthouse tomorrow and sort out a marriage?" I asked her. I knew it wasn't the most romantic proposal a man ever gave a woman—heck, I didn't even have a ring—but she was so strung out that I thought making a big deal out of it all would make her worse.

"I don't know," she whispered.

"Ten minutes ago you said you loved me. Now you don't know?" I said.

"No! I know I love you. I don't know if I can marry you," she said.

"Well, you'll be thrown on a plane back to London if you don't," I said.

"Cardiff Airport is closer to Bristol and it has quite a few long-haul flights," she countered churlishly.

"Young lady, you're going to explain yourself," I said.

"Well, Cardiff is just up the road, but London's hours away…" She seemed to be purposely taking it the wrong way. Was she rooting for a spanking?

"I'm going to count to three, Miss Sutton. Start talking about what's got you so riled up or I'm going to put you straight over my knee," I said. "One."

She looked at me and clammed up again.

"Two."

I raised an eyebrow.

"Th—"

"Okay! I'll tell you." she blurted. "But don't hate me."

"Why would I hate you?" I asked.

"I don't know. Blokes seem to when you let them down about relationships," she said. "I can't marry you because… I don't know how to balance this with my career plan and travel thoughts. I have no idea if we're even going to last or how we could make it work when I have no intention of sacrificing my dreams. Not because I don't like you or anything, but I just don't know you well enough. I've been here three weeks—that's hardly any time at all. I don't even know if you had any childhood pets—"

"Buster. He was a golden retriever. My dad got him when I was four. He died of old age when I was in Iraq in 2003," I said.

"Or who your first date was—"

"Louisa. I liked her so much I married her," I said.

"Or … or… your favorite flavor of ice cream!" She seemed to be losing steam.

"Mint choc chip,"

"Really? That's mine too!" she said. "But that's not the point!"

"Of course it's the point," I said. "Sure, we need to get to know each other some, who doesn't? But if I love you and you love me, that'll all come with time. You need to stop over-complicating everything."

"I don't want to be your ball and chain," she said in a small voice. When I stared at her blankly, she clarified, "I don't want to tie you down. While I get my shit together—my degree, my career and all that, I mean."

"Is that the technical term?" I asked. It elicited a small smile. "I don't want to tie you down either. Literally or figuratively. Well, actually, maybe literally. That depends on you. I know this is all a big deal, you're young, you're carefree, you've got the whole world ahead of you… but I like you, you like me, why shouldn't we be happy together?" I looked into her eyes, but couldn't see the reassurance I sought. "Damnit, Isabel, what else can I do to show you I love you?"

She stared at me for a long minute then started crying again. I sighed. Crying women had never been my forté.

"There's more to this, isn't there? I need you to tell me or I can't fix it for you," I said.

CHAPTER EIGHT

For goodness' sake, now he wanted me to bare my soul to him? There was so much I was holding on to. What would happen if it all came pouring out at once?

I wondered where to start.

"Look here, I've never been in trouble with the law before, and right now I feel like a bloody common criminal. More than that, I feel like America just doesn't want me here," I said. "And, due to the aforementioned not having been in legal problems before, I get the strong feeling that I should just leave quietly without causing a fuss. But you're going out of your way to get me to stay and that puts a lot of pressure on me to live up to your expectations. The fact of the matter is, I just don't want to make a marriage decision based upon my immigration status."

Nate stared at the carpet for several long seconds.

"I thought we had something special going on here," he said. His voice... how had I hurt him so much with a few dozen words?

"Me too," I said.

He started to laugh, his deep baritone chortle.

"What?" I asked.

"You've got to laugh at this situation, Isabel! If you like

84

me and I like you, then what's the problem?" he asked, the remains of a smile still glimmering in his eyes.

"I wanted to have a career in anthropology so I can travel the world," I explained. "And you—you've already done all that. You're looking to settle down and do your farming."

Next he said something that surprised me.

"What makes you think that settling down and traveling and having a career are mutually exclusive?"

"Well... aren't they?" I asked in disbelief.

He put his coffee down and drew me up into his arms.

I felt so safe there, like it was the most perfect place in the world.

"Of course not, Miss Sutton," he replied.

"But what about the boys?" I asked. He couldn't leave them with his parents to go traveling with me, could he?

"You remember how I told you I wanted to get a yacht, and you said you'd always dreamed of traveling the world on a boat, then we talked about how you might decorate it? Let's make it happen. I've wanted to do it for years, but Louisa didn't want to, and as a single parent, I just couldn't see it working out. I don't suppose you'd be interested in finding out whether it's possible to be self-sufficient at sea? Would that be enough traveling the world for you? Or did your dream specifically include seeing the insides of office blocks the world over?" he asked. I had to admit, he had a point. Why go to Hong Kong to sit in a three by four when I could do that at home?

"What about your farm?" I asked.

"I can sell the farm to pay for the yacht," he said.

"You can't put goats and chickens on a yacht," I pointed out.

"No, I'd have to sell the goats and chickens too. And the truck," he said. "I'd have to throw out most of my possessions too. I've been meaning to clear out the attic for years."

I pulled back and stared at Nate for a good while. Was

he serious? Did he really want me on his yacht? How would I finish my Master's degree?

"So what do you say you and me get married, sell the homestead, buy a yacht, and go do some traveling, Miss Sutton?" he asked me.

I was starting to believe that he was serious. It would certainly solve all my immediate problems. Was it a risk? Of course. But part of what had attracted me to anthropology was the risk. The adventure. And part of what had attracted me to Nate was that he made me feel so safe, so cared for, so looked after, even when I was making his dinner. There was no way I was going to try to explain that to my mother.

Going around the world with Nate would be the best of everything.

"Yes. Okay then. Yes," I said.

He squeezed me tighter.

"You sure?" he asked. "You'd have to do everything I say." A hand went down to my ass.

"Well, when you put it like that, how can I refuse?" I replied.

"I'll have to spank you whenever you misbehave," he murmured into my ear.

My knickers were sopping just thinking about it.

"I'm counting on it," I replied.

• • • • • • •

Assured that my Isabel was going to stay, I was on top of the world. I wanted to make her mine again. I released her from the embrace and took her hand.

"Come with me," I said, taking her upstairs.

I closed the bedroom door behind us.

"Take your clothes off and sit on the edge of the bed please, Isabel," I said. My cock was hardening as I thought about what I planned to do to her.

I watched her undress while I took my trousers off.

"Open your mouth, please."

She didn't hesitate. She wanted this as much as I did—maybe more.

I pushed my cock between those waiting, parted lips, and reveled in the feeling of Isabel's tiny tongue massaging my cock, her lips holding it tight, as I stood still while she sucked on it.

She was good, and I felt myself close to coming a lot sooner than I'd expected.

I pulled out, enjoying the look of disappointment on her face as she relinquished my cock.

"On all fours and turn around," I said, remembering why I'd raised the height of the bed frame. A glistening pussy entrance awaited me; there was no doubt that she wanted to feel me inside her.

"You're very turned on for someone who not five minutes ago was trying to convince me not to marry her," I teased.

I gave her soft butt cheeks some well-deserved spanks. She moaned in response.

Positioning the head of my cock at her entrance, I spanked her a couple more times. Her pussy seemed to kind of twitch of its own accord. I pushed into her, savoring the creamy smooth feel of her pussy. It was divine.

I pulled out again, then pushed back in deeply, mesmerized by the slick sheath surrounding my cock. Spurred on by the noises she was making, I took her harder, holding onto her hips and pulling her back so I would penetrate her deeply. She tightened around me and I figured she was just about ready to come, so I pulled out of her.

• • • • • • •

I pouted.

Just as I was about to explode into a million pieces of glittering mica, he pulled out.

"What was that for?" I asked. "I was about to finish."

"It's not going to be that easy now, Miss Sutton," he

said.

I loved when he called me that, it was so gallant and… manly.

"Why not? I want to come!" I said; the need was urgent. I felt, to put it in the vulgar tongue, like a bitch in heat.

"'I want' doesn't get," he said teasingly. He pumped his cock idly as he looked down at my naked body, and I could tell he was highly amused by the situation.

"What do you want?" I asked him suspiciously.

"That's better," he said. "I want you to beg me for it."

I stared at him for a moment.

"Are you having a laugh?" I asked.

"Nope, deadly serious," he said. The glint in his eye told me this was all fun and games but he might spank me in the immediate future. I liked that possibility.

"What's to stop me from finishing myself off?" I asked, raising an eyebrow.

He leaned in and inhaled the scent of my hair. I always used a tropical fruit-scented shampoo, and he seemed to like the way it smelled. He murmured in my ear.

"Not a damn thing. But I know that right now, your whole body is aching for me to fuck you hard, while you come, screaming and writhing on my hard cock."

How did he know? I wanted him so much right now.

"Please, can I … um… come on your … um… with you inside me?" I asked, feeling my pussy get even wetter when I heard myself say those words.

"Now, c'mon, there's nothing to be embarrassed about. An articulate young lady like you can ask me better'n that," he said.

Oh, God, I yearned to feel him in me again.

I needed him so much, I'd sing 'God Save The Queen' right now if he cared to hear it. He could have anything he wanted, and more.

"Please, Nate, can I come on your cock?" I asked again. Just saying the words aloud turned me on more than ever.

He ran a finger down my back.

"Of course you can, Isabel."

He took me from behind again, and this time with a vigorous fervor that proved how much he wanted me. A hand stroked my mound and I cried out in surprise. The hand seemed to stay where it was, stroking me, while I braced myself with my arms and Nate thrust hard inside me.

I heard the bed springs sproinging and the headboard hitting the wall as he claimed me in the way I needed. I came, feeling like I'd been swimming underwater and now broke the surface, back arched, my red hair flung back; somehow I was still balancing as I remained rigid for several seconds.

He pulled out.

"What are you doing?" I asked. I was sure he hadn't come yet.

"Just relax," he said, stroking the back of my neck. He never said that before anything relaxing was about to happen. Sure enough, I felt his finger dive into my ridiculously wet pussy, then he removed it and pressed it against my back entrance, which resisted him.

"Relax into it for me; remember how good it felt last time."

The memory of holding onto the bath taps while he explored my arse with his finger made me open a bit more, and his finger now slid inside gently, feeling so good as he gently stroked my least-used nerve endings.

"That's it, Isabel, you're doing swell." He pressed a second finger against the entrance, and my eyes widened as I contemplated this new, filling feeling. I shouldn't have worried; Nate knew exactly what he was doing and soon I was leaning into it as he moved in and out of me. A few seconds later, I gasped as his cock pressed into my pussy again, and what with the two fingers as well, I was on my way to another cracking orgasm.

"Good girl, Isabel," Nate encouraged, and his voice and the reminder that it was him inside me, his huge cock filling my pussy while his fingers filled my arse, pushed me over the edge and I screamed into the mattress as he continued to press into me. I felt my muscles clench down on his fingers as the sizzling tingle in the nerve endings added to the delicious feeling of his cock, until soon I was lost in my own little world of glowing warmth.

Behind me, I felt Nate drive into me a couple more times, then he came, with a slight growl, gripping my hips as he filled me with his seed, making me tremble with an intense aftershock that could have been an orgasm in its own right. Everything just felt so perfect.

CHAPTER NINE

"Are you sure there should be so many flowers?" I asked my dad as I fastened the cufflinks, the finishing touch to my best suit.

"Yep. Son, never underestimate the amount of flowers a woman wants at her wedding. They're famous for it. Flowers in their hands, in their hair, on their dresses, in the lapels of all the menfolk... there ain't nowhere a woman won't put a flower on her wedding day."

My dad's attempt at a dirty joke was met with a slight chuckle. He was a good guy with all the right values, and I couldn't fault the way he and my mother had raised me, but no man wants to hear their honest-to-goodness parents making ribald jokes about their bride.

Especially not on their wedding day.

We didn't have many guests; the trouble with going away to war for eight years is that you come back to find all the friends who stayed at home moved on, and all the friends who stayed in the forces get posted elsewhere, so it makes it difficult to summon your friends to your last-minute wedding, unless it's remotely near where they're currently stationed. All I'd received from the hasty email invites we'd had to rely on was a lot of "sorry, I'm posted to

Hawaii/Alaska/the Middle East and can't get leave."

Our parents and my kids were the only ones who'd arrived so far—Isabel's parents had even flown out from England.

I went outside to the makeshift aisle in the garden. It was only about six feet long because that was as many chairs as we'd needed. The seats were decorated with garlands of flowers and long interwoven Michaelmas daisy chains marked out the short aisle.

At the end of the aisle, there was an archway covered in flowers, under which the officiant waited.

I was pleased to see a couple of old friends had made it after all. It was good to see their faces.

Isabel appeared at the kitchen door, and I caught my breath. I'd never seen anyone so beautiful. Her dress was stunning—floor length with a figure-hugging satin skirt, a deep plunging neckline with a shaped bodice over the top, and sparkling sequins all over it to catch the sunlight. The white of the dress contrasted with her auburn hair, giving the visual effect that she might be an elf. It suited her. Over the top, she wore a veil that trailed along the floor behind her. Cathedral length, she'd called it. I tried to forget that her outfit had cost as much as a small church. The overall effect was incredible. I could hardly believe that in a few minutes' time she'd be all mine.

The warm breeze gently rustled her hair under the veil. She linked arms with her father before walking to the short aisle where I awaited her. Her father passed her over to me and patted me on the shoulder.

"Take good care of her," he said, getting misty-eyed as he passed me to sit down.

"Are you ready, Isabel?" I asked her.

She looked at me and nodded.

We stepped out onto our floral aisle, and slowly walked to the archway of flowers. The officiant greeted us with a smile.

"Marriage is a sacred and special moment in two

people's lives. This wedding today is a joining, legally, of two souls that have already become entwined, inextricably, by the powerful bonds of love, and we are all gathered here today to bear witness to this momentous occasion when they publicly pledge their commitment to one another," she said. "Do you, Nathaniel Byrne, take this woman, Isabel Sutton, who stands before you, to be your lawfully wedded wife?"

"I do," I said proudly.

"And do you, Isabel Sutton, take this man, Nathaniel Byrne, who stands before you, to be your lawfully wedded husband?"

Isabel hesitated for a split second, and I had this terrible moment where I thought she was going to refuse me. Then, the sun came out as she smiled broadly and looked up to me.

"I do," she said.

"Then if there are no objections, it is time to exchange the rings," she said. "The ring is an ancient symbol of love and commitment; its shape is eternal, perfect, showing the never-ending ties between husband and wife. The rings exchanged today are a lasting and visual reminder of that which these two people share. Where are the rings?"

My father came forward and presented me with a ring box, which held a white gold band chosen by Isabel. I took her left hand and placed the modest band at the tip of her finger.

"Repeat after me: With this ring, I thee wed," the officiant said.

"With this ring, I thee wed," I said, pushing the ring onto Isabel's finger.

My father pulled out another box out and presented it to my imminent wife.

She took out the rose gold ring that I'd chosen and put it to my fingertip.

"With this ring, I thee wed," Isabel said, sliding the ring to the base of my finger.

"In which case, before all assembled here and the state of California, I do pronounce you both husband and wife," the officiant said. "You may now kiss the bride."

I took her face in my hands, looked into her emerald eyes, leaned in and kissed her, hearing the gentle thud of her bouquet hitting the floor as she dropped it in the moment. My tongue found hers and I tasted her sweet essence, that musky chocolate flavor that she seemed to radiate. The smell of the daisies seemed to complement her taste perfectly. Her hair felt bunny-soft under my fingertips. As the kiss went on, I could see and feel her blushing.

When the kiss ended, everyone stood up and broke into spontaneous applause.

EPILOGUE

Six months later

As I stared out across the endless Pacific Ocean, I could comprehensively see why, throughout history, people had thought the world was flat. It was hard to imagine that anything lay beyond that distant horizon. I felt so humbled to be here.

It had taken me a couple of weeks to find my sea legs, since my only seafaring experience before today had been a few trips on the Dover-Calais route on a ferry across the Channel as a child, when (aside from that one year we went to Skegness) my dad had taken us on the annual family camping trip to France every August. Usually it had been calm on that ferry, but forty minutes on even the most stormy trip had been nothing compared to spending all day every day with the motion of a yacht on an open ocean.

I'd actually wondered whether I'd have to call it all off and find some dry land from which to await Nate and the boys, but since the ship obviously didn't have an airport, that would have been somewhat difficult when we were already five hundred miles off the coast of California. To say it had been bloody awful was an understatement.

Thankfully, even the occasional relapses of nausea had cleared up after a fortnight and I began to enjoy the trip. True to his word, Nate had let me paint the interior aquamarine, although the carpets were all dark red, presumably so they didn't show stains if he spilled wine on them.

I was glad that Immigration had now backed off, after taking us to separate rooms and giving us the Spanish Inquisition about each other's lives, families, and, bizarrely, each other's names. That had made me burst out laughing but the stern immigration official hadn't seen the funny side. Apparently there are people out there who don't know the name of the person they're marrying. Who knew?

We had put down anchor in the Pacific somewhere. I'd just tucked the boys into their bunks and Nate had requested my presence on the deck, but then he'd been delayed by something to do with one of the batteries the yacht got her power from.

"Is there something you need to tell me, young lady?" Nate's voice carried across from the hatch as he emerged and came toward me. There was something unfamiliar in his hand.

"Um… I forgot to put the leftovers in the fridge again," I said. "Oops."

"Third time in two weeks, Mrs. Byrne. What did I say after the second time?" Nate prompted. I loved it when he called me Mrs. Byrne.

"That you were going to spank me soundly if I did it again," I said. "But I didn't think you *meant* it."

"Now you know better. I'm afraid you leave me no choice, young lady. We can't afford to waste food when we're at sea. If we run out while we're out here, we starve."

He sat in the captain's chair and swiveled it round so his back was to the wheel. He tended to stand when he steered anyway, but the chair was the perfect height for this.

Hesitantly, but gushing into my knickers, I stepped toward him and let him guide me over his knee.

He rubbed my bottom over my thin summery skirt, and I purred like a tame kitten.

"Now, Mrs. Byrne, I'm going to spank every inch of your naughty ass until it turns red. I might even have to go extra long, since it's hard to pick out colors in the moonlight." His voice was stern and I felt reassured in his strong hands that although I'd been bad, and the spanking was going to hurt, it would make me feel better afterwards; *he* would make it all better.

He knew he had this power over me and he loved it as much as I did.

My skirt was pulled back, my knickers removed.

His hands caressed my bare bottom as I studied the deck in the silver moonlight.

He brought his hand down on my right cheek and I wiggled a bit.

"Stop struggling or I'll add extras with my belt," he said. It wasn't an empty threat, so I behaved.

He brought his hand down again, this time on my left cheek, then several blows on my sit spot. After that I think he was just filling in the empty space on his canvas.

Soon, I was breathing heavily and my arousal was probably visible to the astronauts in space. He kept spanking me.

"Please, I'm really sorry, I promise I won't do it again," I implored him. "You can let me go now, I've learned my lesson."

"This isn't for what you will do; it's for what you already did. Three good meals, each for four people, have been wasted this week. You need to ensure it never happens again, but you're getting this full spanking anyway, regardless of what you promise not to do." Nate said sternly.

He continued spanking, building up to harder smacks, and soon I was crying.

It wasn't long after that he stopped, caressed my bottom lightly with his big fingers, then tipped me upright and held me.

He gazed into my eyes, as he always liked to after a spanking, and brushed the tears away.

"All is forgiven," he said. "Now I want you to remove your dress and bend over the safety rail at the prow, holding it tight."

I did as he told me, feeling my red bottom glowing in the night.

Who needed lanterns?

I looked over my shoulder in surprise when he took my right hand and lashed it to the safety rail. *That* was what he'd been carrying when he arrived on deck. He lashed my left hand as well.

"I don't want you going overboard while I have my way with you," he murmured in my ear.

The idea that he'd thought about that turned me on more than the rope itself, which was merely a precaution to my mind. Although, I realized, being lashed to the rail around the prow like this did have the side effect of making it impossible to escape. Not that there was any risk of that. He was stuck with me now, for as long as he wanted, as long as he loved me and spanked me and… well, you get the point.

He put a hand to my entrance and withdrew it again.

"You, young lady, are dripping wet. There's only one thing to do. I am going to fuck you in both your holes."

With that, a hand stroked my most delicate clit and I opened myself to him. He pushed inside me and penetrated me to my core. A little moan escaped my lips. I always felt like a missing jigsaw piece had been replaced when he did this. It was a wonderful feeling. He withdrew slightly, but not fully, and I waited to see what he was going to do next. Pressing in deeply again, he made me cry out once more. His cold skin hit my burning, freshly spanked bum and it was delicious. Unable to really move from my position, I stayed in place, gazing at the midnight ocean as Nate took me, lovingly, above the salty waves lapping against the boat. His movements got quicker as all I could do was take him, getting closer to my own climax.

As I was close to coming, he eased his cock out and positioned it at my other entrance. My excitement was palpable. There was a bit of pressure as he pushed into my arse. I was always amazed that he seemed to fit without any pain. He stayed still a few seconds, allowing me to adjust, then began to slowly move in and out, touching against those oh-so-sensitive nerve endings that made me come the hardest. A finger dipped into my pussy, followed by a second. His thumb stroked my clit and I moaned. I was so full, and it felt so good!

"Somebody's excited to have me in her ass," Nate said, and I nodded emphatically. Between the fingers in my pussy and his cock in my derriere, not to mention the attention he was giving to my little clit, I very rapidly built to the edge. I turned my head back to him.

"Please, can I come?" I asked him. It always thrilled me to say those words, to place my orgasm directly in his capable hands.

"Let's see… hot spanked bottom, dripping wet pussy, my hard cock inside you… yes, you are allowed to come."

He always seemed to know exactly the right words to tip me into infinity, as I screamed my finale across the ocean, gripping the handrail for all I was worth, flexing my leg muscles, arching my back like a real figurehead, the sea breeze playing against my bare nipples.

With a cry, I felt rather than heard Nate's finish. His cock pulsed inside me, filling me once more with his seed, renewing his claim on me, reminding me that I was his. I loved knowing I'd helped him come.

He unfastened me and we both sort of collapsed on the deck, the waves splashing against the side of the bobbing yacht, anchored in the middle of nowhere. Above us, the stars watched impartially, neither casting judgment nor encouragement, and the moon lit our naked bodies as we glistened with sweat, utterly shagged out.

I lay with my head on his chest.

"So… Hawaii University for a September start?" he reminded me, stroking my hair with his free hand as he held me close with the other.

"Yep," I replied.

"Were they good about the credit transfer?" he asked.

"Oh, I forgot to tell you, they emailed this morning and said that was all sorted. They've even found me a teaching assistant position so I shouldn't run out of money this time," I said. Thank goodness for mobile Internet.

"I hope not—what if you get another job on a farm and meet another strapping young man who spanks you when you're naughty and fucks you when you're good?" he asked.

"Nate!!" I squealed, worried that the boys would hear such foul language coming from their father. "One man taking me in hand is definitely exactly the right amount. If there was another one of you around, I'd never have time to eat, let alone go back to university. How would I *ever* sit down again?" I said. "Besides, aren't we going to park the boat in a marina and live on it still for the year? I was looking forward to occasional sojourns to the other Hawaiian islands."

"We sure are. I was only teasing you," Nate said. He was rather good at that, I thought.

We leaned back a bit and gazed at the stars some more. Had the stars, in their permanent, phosphorescent points of vantage, known that my life was going to turn out like this? It seemed like a lifetime had passed since I'd replied to that ad on Craigslist. I was a different person now—more confident, happier, less uncertain about what I wanted and needed. If the stars had told me my future all those months ago, I would have been afraid, would have tried to avoid it, since I didn't know any better. On reflection, I thought, it was a bloody good thing that they had remained silent on the matter.

THE END

Made in the USA
San Bernardino, CA
23 May 2017